TALES OLDER THAN TIME

Tales Older Than Time

A COLLECTION OF SHORT STORIES SET IN THE PAST

Dustin Lowe

Dustin Lowe Publishing

Contents

1	The Mail Guards Story	1
2	The Great Sea Serpent	17
3	An Errand at Midnight	23
4	Aunt Eliza's Ghost Story	33
5	The Suicide of the Pont Neuf	38
6	Life and Fortune Lost on the Race Course	46
7	Gideon Gadsby's Christmas	54
8	The Photograph Mystery	61
9	Story of the Whale	68
10	A Vision of Hanging	75
11	Judge and Executioner	79
12	The Cuckoo's Song	87

1

The Mail Guards Story

Reader, have you ever been obliged to wait at a small country railway station for an early train? If you have not, you have not experienced the highest point of human misery. But when, as was my case last year, you have left a jolly party, driven five miles to catch the mail at two a.m. and found, on your arrival at the station, not that the train had gone, for that would be a relief, but that you had mistaken the time and had got three-quarters of an hour to wait, your lot is not an enviable one. So I thought as I stamped up and down the ill-lit platform, and gazed into the darkness beyond, which was only broken by the dim and misty light of the "distance" signal, some hundred yards down the line. The occasional barking of a house dog alone broke the stillness, except now and then the autumn breeze played in a wailing tone on the telegraph wires over my head. As I paced up and down to warm my feet, I felt regularly "savage" that the solicitations of the company assembled at the Beeches had induced me to forego that last waltz with Minnie Cameron, and hurry to the station.

I had been staying for the past fortnight at the house of a relative and what with shooting, fishing, and (must I confess it) occasionally flirting with the blue-eyed Minnie, the days had passed rapidly; and when recalled to London by my father's business-like letter, which hinted at some impending calamity connected with our firm, I could not believe that my leave had so nearly expired. There was no help for it and go I must. My relatives appeared as sorry as I was when I announced my intended departure and I fancy I could discern traces of tears in Minnie's sunny eyes as I bade her farewell in the hall that evening, bearing with me a shining tress of her flaxen hair, and a hasty kiss, as souvenirs of my visit.

Under such circumstances as I have described the reader will easily imagine I was not in a particularly cheerful frame of mind on the night, or rather morning, in question. I sauntered into the dreary waiting room, and lighted a cigar, seated myself in front of the expiring fire, which I was even denied the amusement of stirring, the authorities having carried away the fire irons. Placing my feet upon the fender, I lay back in my chair, and, as most men would have done, began to ruminate upon the events of the past fortnight, and— Minnie!

After a time, I roused myself, and attempted to reperuse my father's letter and then I fell fast asleep. How long I slept I cannot say, probably about five minutes, but it seemed an eternity, when I was aroused by the creaking of the breaks of a train. I stood up and rushed blindly to the door, fancying that the mail had come up, when I came in violent contact with a guard, who was entering at the same moment as I was making a hurried exit.

"Beg your pardon, sir," said the polite official; "what is the matter?"

"My train is going, I think." said I.

"It's only for goods and cattle, sir," replied my companion, "The up-mail ain't due for nearly twenty minutes yet."

"Confound it!" I muttered; "why did it wake me, then?" And I returned to the fireplace.

"Cold night, sir," remarked the guard as he came towards me.

"Yes," I said, "and a wretched fire, too."

"I think we can mend that, at any rate," he said; and, leaving the room, he returned in a few minutes, accompanied by an individual whom I rightly conjectured to be the stoker of the goods train, carrying a large shovelful of live coals, which, placed upon the cinders, soon improved our fire, and gave quite a cheerful aspect to the dingy apartment.

"Thank ye, Jim," said the guard as the stoker departed. "Now, sir, that's an improvement, ain't it?" He added cheerfully.

"It is, indeed," I replied, "and I am much obliged to you for procuring the coals."

"Don't mention it, sir," was the reply, "One must do something when one has to wait, you know."

"How long do you remain here," I asked.

"Till 3:40, sir. I take up the mail," was the reply.

"Oh, indeed." I said.

"Yes, sir. I'm on this job all this month." And as he spoke

the guard drew a pipe from his pocket and having filled and lit it, he began to smoke in silence.

"Have you been long on this line?" I asked after a pause.

"Well, sir, about three years and on the mail duty, on and off, about one. I'm a regular man of letters," he added with a grin. I laughed and he continued. "I had letters on my collar when I was in the police. And now that I am a guard, I look after the letters."

Having made these remarks in a jocular tone, my companion gave me a knowing nod, and pulled away at his pipe with greater vigor than before. I was much amused at his answer and asked him what he meant by having letters on his collar.

"I wasn't always a guard, sir," he said. "I was once in the police, and it was through being a detective that I got to be employed on this line."

"I suppose you didn't like the police, then?" I said.

"Well, sir, not much, though at times it was pretty good, and we had some jolly business." He continued, "with a good scent it's almost as excitin' as fox-huntin'; for some of those fellows are as cunnin' as foxes, every bit. It was through a robbery and a bit of paper that I was made a guard, as I am now."

"How was that?" I asked, catching at the idea of a story to beguile the time. "I should like to hear a bit of your experience as a detective."

"It ain't much of a story, sir. But I'll tell it to you with pleasure," and taking a few rapid puffs at his pipe, the guard commenced.

"It was about two years ago, and there had been a great

robbery in the city; the thieves had got away, so we was all obliged to keep our eyes open and our wits about us, for, though we had some suspicions, there was no real clues to go upon; it was mostly guesswork. Two or three men were arrested, but nothing was ever proved against them, so they was let go, of course. Nothing ever transpired regarding the robbery, and it was almost forgotten, except by some of us detectives, for a reward of £500 had been offered, and we was, of course, anxious to catch the men, not just for the money but the credit as well. I wasn't half satisfied about one of the men who had been arrested, and whose name was Dover. He and another was always together and we in the force nick-named them Chatham and Dover, in consequence. We had 'Chatham' (whose real name was Byles) come in, but nothing turned up.

"However, one night after the whole business had blown over a bit, I thought I'd have a look after Dover; so, I goes to where I was sure to find him or his pal, in an out-of-the-way place near Field Lane. When the door was opened, I saw as the woman was a new hand and didn't know me. So, I asked if Dover was in. 'No,' says she, 'he's gone out of town.'

"'In which direction?' I says. She pointed upwards, which meant north. 'Indeed,' says I. 'Well, tell him Mr. Moss wants to see him as soon as he returns.'

"'All right,' says she, and shuts the door.

"I got to thinking, I've not done a bad stroke of business this evening. Mr. Moss and I will settle our little account now; so, I went quietly home. Next afternoon, just after dinner, a message comes in from the bank for Mr. Tremble, our inspector. Telling me to be ready in case of bein' wanted. Off he goes, and in about an hour he came back and said, 'We've got a job tonight,' he says, 'for a party has written another gentleman's name by mistake and bolted with a large sum of money and his young woman to America.' We had to start that evening by the nine o' clock train for Liverpool, which we did, and arrived there about four the next morning. We immediately put ourselves in communication with the local authorities and searched several outgoing ships, but without any success.

"Just as we were leaving one of the vessels, the captain said to me: 'It's a pity you didn't know a little sooner; an American barque sailed yesterday's tide for New York.'

"'The deuce it did,' says Mr. Tremble.

"'Yes,' says the captain; 'and you may depend upon it your man was off in that vessel.'

"'We're done, then,' says Mr. Tremble.

"'Well,' says I, ' I don't see that, by no means. When does the mail go?' I asked the captain.

"'It's gone,' says he; 'went last night.'

"'That's no good, then,' says Mr. Tremble. And he was very angry at bein' done.

"'I think, Mr. Tremble,' I says, as we walked away, 'I think we can catch him yet.'

"'How?' says Mr. Tremble.

"'Let us take the steamer to Dublin this afternoon and go by the mail tram to Queenstown; we can catch the steamer there and pin your man in New York.'

"'I declare, we will,' says Mr. Tremble, 'that's a good idea; only I'm afraid I shall have to go alone, for you will be wanted in London, you know, next week.' I had forgotten that and was very much disappointed at not being able to accompany Mr. Tremble to New York.

"'However,' says he, 'I'll not forget you when I come back.' And in order to arrange our plans and have some breakfast, we returned to the railway station. I saw Mr. Tremble off for Hollyhead and felt very much annoyed at not being able to go with him, though, had I known it was the best thing that ever happened to me, I shouldn't have felt so sulky. As the boat left the landing stage, I turned into the street and walked about until I saw a great crowd opposite a jeweler's shop. I asked a bystander, and he told me that an immense amount of jewelry had been stolen the previous night, and there was no trace of the robber. 'Ho, ho!' I thought. And I asked to see the owner of the shop. Telling him who I was, I requested to see some traces of the thief's work for, sir, some men work exactly the same way at all their 'cracks,' and you can tell their 'handwriting' after a bit of practice.

"I therefore examined the place, and, as I suspected, found that this robbery had been done in a similar way to the one in London. For it had occurred to me that Mr. Dover had not left London for nothing, and now I was pretty sure that he and his 'pals' had done this job as well. After making my inspection and asking the proprietor to say nothing about my visit, I returned to Lime Street station.

"I then found that I could return to London by a slow train at one o'clock, which, as I had nothing to do in Liverpool, I preferred to take rather than wait for the 2:45 express. I was in better spirits now than I had been and as I entered the train, I made up my mind to look for Dover in London, which I never doubted he had returned, for of all hiding places, sir, London is the best. So, I made myself as comfortable as possible. Nothing happened till, as we were nearing Stafford, a bit of paper was blown into my face; and as I, out of mere curiosity, stooped to pick it up from the seat where it had fallen, two other and larger pieces came in and fell on the floor.

"There was no one else in the compartment, so I put the scraps together just to see what I could make out of them and to my astonishment I read:

"'I will be at ＿＿two o'clock＿＿ you do it. —Dover.'"

"That was all. The last words, on the smallest bit of paper, I didn't care for; but the other parts made my heart jump when I read them, for I made sure that I should now catch Mr. Dover for the robbery at Liverpool. The instant the train stopped, out I jumped, and began looking into the carriages as I passed, pretending I had lost something. At last, I came to a carriage near the engine (a second-class); on the flooring of which I could see several bits of paper, and upon going on I found (for the carriage was empty); an envelope, addressed to some place in Camden Town, in the same handwriting as was on the bits I had.

"While I was examining the envelope, I saw three men coming from the refreshment room in the direction of the carriage, so I seated myself in a corner next to the door and shut my eyes. I was more than ever convinced that I now had a clue to the Liverpool job, and I determined to keep my eye on the former occupants of the carriage, who now returned to their seats.

"The smell of rum which pervaded the compartment, convinced me that they had been indulging pretty freely, and when they were in earnest conversation, I opened my eye. Sitting nearly opposite to me was Dover himself; the other men I did not know. Before the train got to Rugby, they were all fast asleep; as soon as we stopped, out I jumped and left them snoring."

"You went for assistance I suppose," I said.

"No, sir," replied the guard, with a knowing wink, "I wanted them in London, not Rugby; for, you see, by staying on the train I might have excited suspicion, and my birds would've flown. No, sir; London was their destination, and I could catch them on their arrival."

"Well," I said, "but you left the train, you say."

"I did, sir; for it occurred to me that the 3:45 express from Liverpool was due, and I knew that it left Rugby a few minutes before the train in which Dover and his friends were. Just as I got out and had shut the door, I had the satisfaction of seeing the train shunting, to make room for the express, which came up a few minutes after. I was soon on my road to London, where I arrived about nine o'clock.

"I had just an hour and a half to make my arrangements, and while my men were quietly jogging along near Tring in the slow train, I was soon in possession of the necessary authority and, taking two of our men with me, I returned to Euston Square. We had to wait some time, but the train at last arrived, and I led the way to the carriage in which I had left Dover and his associates. They were just getting out as we reached them, and a gentle grasp on the collar and a word in the ear, soon reduced them to a terrified silence. Their baggage was also seized, and in a portmanteau was found a quantity of the jewelry which had been stolen in Liverpool.

"We had them up next day and they were fully committed. At the trial one of them turned evidence, and by those means the city burglary was proved against them. The rewards were paid over to me after the trial, and I was very much complimented by the judges on the manner in which I had managed the capture."

"I think you quite deserved the rewards," I said. "But what became of the inspector?"

"Oh, Mr. Tremble, sir. He went across, as I had told him by the mail from Queenstown and got to America the day before the ship in which the forger was. He boarded every ship, and from the description he had received he caught him before he went on shore. There was no doubt about him, for some of the identical notes which had been issued in London were found upon him.

"Mr. Tremble didn't bring him back, sir; he only took possession of the money; for he thought it would cost more to bring him home and prosecute than to leave him where he was. The bank gentleman said he was quite right and gave him two hundred and fifty dollars for his trouble. When he returned to England, one of the directors at the bank, who was our chairman, was complimenting Mr. Tremble upon going to Ireland— and then Mr. Tremble spoke up for me; and knowin' as I didn't care for the force, he told the gentleman so, and he, after a time, offered me the place I have now, with a prospect of a rise if I behaved myself. So, you see sir, it was as I said, all through a torn piece of a letter had I gotten to be a mail guard."

"I am very much obliged to you," I said, "for your narrative has amused me very much, indeed."

"I am very glad to hear it, sir," replied the ex-detective, "and you'll excuse me, sir but I think I've seen you before."

"Very likely," I said, laughing, "your experience has doubtless led you across my path." "Ay, I thought as much, sir," said the guard; "I saw you when the chairman offered me the post I have. I remember you was comin' in as I left the bank."

"I dare say I did, for my father sees a great many people at the bank," I said.

"Is your father, Mr. George Somerville? *The* Mr. Somerville? The chairman?"

"Yes," said I; "I have just been at my uncle's house now, and am on my way to London, where my father is at present."

"Well, ain't that curious, sir," said the guard, touching his cap, "that I should see you here this evening. I'm proud to have met you, sir."

I replied and the guard, running to the door, exclaimed, "Here's the mail, sir; if you'll show me your things, I'll see that they are all right." And once more touching his cap, he withdrew. The mail soon drew up and, having been comfortably bestowed by the guard, we spun over the distance that lay between here and the metropolis, I pondered on the singular story I had heard until I fell into a doze, from which I was not thoroughly awakened until the train stopped to take tickets.

We were soon afterward at the station, and as I stepped out of the carriage, I found the guard ready to assist me. He soon extricated my portmanteau from the heap at the end of the platform and insisted upon carrying it to the entrance of the station, for, strange as it may appear, there were no cabs in attendance that morning. As we emerged into the street a Hansom cab drew up close to the departure entrance and the guard hailing the driver, we waited until the fare had alighted.

I was astonished to find that the gentleman who was about to take his departure this early from London was none other than my father's confidential clerk, respecting whom my father had already communicated his suspicions in the letter I had received the morning before. I stared at the sudden appearance of the very person whose affairs I had come to London to investigate and followed his retreating figure with so earnest a gaze that the guard, who had been observing me closely, said:

"Beg pardon, sir; do you know that gentleman?"

"Certainly, I do," I replied, "I've come to town on his account; Mr. Barton is my father's confidential clerk. But I'm afraid all is not quite right," I added, thoughtfully, and in an undertone.

"I suspect there's a little game," said the guard; "the man that gone in there was called Byles three year ago."

I was struck with astonishment at this remark and asked my companion if he were certain that the so-called Barton was in reality Byles, alias Chatham.

"As certain as I stand here," replied the guard, "and take my word for it, sir, he's up to no good. If you don't think me presumin', I should like to hear what's up."

"Well," I said, " the matter is a confidential one; but I may tell you that we have reason to suspect that Mr. Byles' accounts are in a most unsatisfactory state. Can we not intercept him, for I think he intends to bolt?"

"We shall soon see that, sir," replied the guard, his

detective nature showing for a moment; "he will be easily caught, I reckon."

As he spoke, the ex-policeman led the way to the departure platform. Here, amid the crowd of people who had taken their tickets and were struggling to enter the different carriages, it was no easy matter to recognize Mr. Barton, who had, doubtless, his own reasons for eluding observation; and it was not until five minutes prior to the departure of the train that I observed him ensconced in a corner of a third-class carriage.

"Good morning, Mr. Barton," I said; "you are off early today."

The person addressed changed color as he recognized me; but immediately recovering himself, replied: "Yes, sir. Mr. Somerville wished to see me regarding those bills we hold, as soon as possible and I am on my way down."

"But they are all right," I said, "for my father told me so last week."

"Yes sir," said the clerk; "but my mother is very ill, I fear, and as Mr. Somerville kindly told me to go down to Greenwich, I said I'd do the bills too." And having given vent to this contradictory speech, the clerk blew his nose violently.

The cool way in which this was said, and the curious looks of the other occupants of the compartment at any other time would have quieted my suspicions; but a gentle touch on the arm reminded me of the presence of the guard and I therefore said, loudly, "Oh, you are going to Greenwich."

As I spoke, the guard said suddenly, and touching his cap respectfully, "Beg your pardon sir; did you say you was going to Greenwich?"

"No," I replied, "but this gentleman is," indicating Mr. Barton as I spoke.

"Very sorry," continued the guard, "but he can't go by this train; he must wait for the next train at 8:05. Tickets, please," he added, suddenly opening the door.

All the tickets, with the exception of the clerk's, were immediately produced. "Now, sir, your ticket, please," said the guard.

Thus, brought to bay, Byles had no alternative; as he handed the guard his ticket, and suddenly rising, attempted to leave the carriage, but the detective was too quick for him. Before the clerk's foot had touched the platform, a grasp was laid upon his collar and the carriage door closed.

"I thought as much," said the guard, as he looked at the ticket, hording unhappy Barton all the while; "I thought so. Going abroad was you, sir; but I want you for a moment." He then asked me to open the door, again descended from the carriage, forcing Barton to follow him; when, having stepped down to the platform, he whispered a few words in his ear.

The man grew as pale as death, exclaiming, "I never did! I swear I never did!"

At that moment the whistle sounded, and with a hiss and a scream the train moved away. Life, liberty, hope— all seemed to fade from the unhappy wretch as the carriages passed by and with an almost superhuman effort he wrenched himself from the guards grasp and attempted to open one of the doors of the departing train.

Cries of "Stop him!" were raised by the spectators, while the guard hurried in pursuit, but his efforts were of no avail. Before anyone could seize the fugitive, his foot had slipped, and still clinging to the handle, he was carried along for a few yards and then dashed between the platform and the now rapidly moving train.

A despairing cry and a deep groan were heard even above the rattle of the wheels. The train passed on, leaving the mangled yet still breathing form of the unfortunate clerk stretched across the rails.

Assistance was immediately procured. But it was of no use; death soon put an end to his sufferings; but before he died, the unhappy man confessed his guilt to me and asked my pardon. It appeared he had been induced to embezzle sums of money to repay losses with his old associates, and he had thus been led to return to a path of life which he had intended to quit forever when he entered my father's business.

He had contrived to possess himself in all of about thirty thousand dollars in bills and notes; some of which, to the value of ten thousand dollars, were found upon him. The remainder had been made away with and was never recovered. Having made such arrangements as were necessary, I left the station and proceeded home to communicate to my father the tragic termination of my journey, when I found he had already taken steps for arresting Barton on his appearance in the city, circumstances having arisen which placed his guilt beyond question.

My father was much moved and interested by the details of the death of his unhappy clerk, and by my recital of the circumstances of my meeting with the guard, who had fully repaid the interest my parent had formerly taken in him. The fortunes of our house soon recovered the blow which the misguided Barton had managed to inflict upon our credit. I consider the prosperity of the firm of Somerville & Co. is due to my accidental meeting with, and the story to told me by the mail guard.

2

The Great Sea Serpent

There was a thick bank of clouds on the horizon, and as the sun rose from the sea, behind the dark bank great masses of color— red and blue and yellow— lit up the whole expanse of sky and sea. I was looking at a strange ruddy plot of red on the water right astern when I saw, apparently near the horizon, but in the red blot, a dark moving shadow. It did not seem to move with the other shadows on the sea, and this fixed my attention to it. Soon I saw it was steadily approaching the vessel. I could distinguish no form, only a dark shadow, but I made out certainly that it was advancing toward us and at a great rate.

Fifteen minutes must have passed when I at last became able to distinguish the form of the advancing object. I spoke to the captain afterward as to the distance the object could have been from us when I first distinguished it, and he told me I must have been deceived by the moving lights near the horizon; and he guessed, from what I said, that it was then three or four miles distant. Mistakes of a like nature, he said, are commonly made by the inexperienced. I cannot accurately describe my feelings on beholding that hideous sight. At first, I turned to call out, to bring others to look on with me; but before a cry could pass through my lips, a second feeling of selfishness that I alone saw that fearful thing, seized me, and I turned my eyes again to the sea and kept them there.

Within a hundred feet of the stern of our vessel, not approaching us, but simply following steadily in our wake, was this hideous thing. A great mass of what looked like tangled seaweed, on which a futile attempt at combing had been made, rose out of the water. This mass must have been twenty or thirty feet in length and ten feet in width, and as it came closer it caused a wide ripple in the water that showed there must still be a great part of the creature below the surface. From the center part of this mass, raised just clear above it, and facing the vessel, was a great black head. The top was quite flat, in shape not unlike that of monstrous toad. A thick fringe of coarse, reddish hair hung over the mouth, quite concealing it. But the eyes were the most awful part of this fearful thing. They were placed far apart, at either extremity of the flat head, distant from each other at least three feet.

I must state here that all the passengers and all the crew, except the captain himself, saw the thing afterward, but that they were scarcely two who could agree as to the color and nature of these eyes. I can only, therefore, write as they appeared to me. The eyeballs were enormous; they must have been four or five inches in diameter. They glistened constantly. Everyone knows the extraordinary appearance of a surface covered with small alternate squares of bright red and bright blue, the quivering, uncertain, unfixed look such a surface has, the difficulty, the impossibility experienced by the onlooker to fix the color of any particular square. The eyeballs of this thing has such a quivering, uncertain look; but they were not red, nor blue, in their color; they were of a bright, burningly bright, copper hue; they pained our eyes— and in this we were all agreed— as we looked at them. In the center of each eyeball, a mere speck, but visible from its extreme brightness, was a point of light, of white light. It was impossible to tell whether these points were or were not material points of the eye or merely caused by reflection, but they were clearly defined, and seemed to remain in the same place. The appearance of this extraordinary creature was so new to me, so entirely outside all my previous experience, that I had no preconceived ideas with what to compare it to. The impression it caused was vague and indefinite, and I can only say that it both scared and fascinated me.

I had been so absorbed in the pleasing pain of looking at the thing, that I had quite forgotten the other people on board and was first roused by hearing Captain Davidson step upon the stern by me, gave one look below at the water and then hurriedly went back inside. In a few minutes, every passenger was crowding onto the stern. Exclamations of astonishment broke from all, and then silence fell, as the crowd stared at the hideous creature. The children, at the first sight, ran back below screaming and some refused to come out again onto the deck. Some, however, returned, curiosity overcoming fear. But even these people had a constant tremor of terror and held themselves ready at the first movement of the thing to rush away. I noticed at this time that the captain was not present and turned to an old European sailor by me and asked him to go and tell him.

"Captain won't come out, sir," replied the man. I asked him if the captain was navigating the ship.

"No, he wasn't navigating the ship. He still refuses to come out."

We all remained absorbed in the strange sight till the first breakfast bell rang at 8:30. Up until this time, the thing had kept steadily in our wake, its movement continuing absolutely smooth and constant, and the specks of light in the glaring eyes never changing a hair's breadth from their position.

At breakfast I sat one seat removed from the captain. We began, of course, talking of the thing we had seen, but the captain, for some reason we couldn't understand, seemed to dislike the subject, and we soon abandoned it, falling into absolute silence since we couldn't talk about anything else. When we went on deck again— we only spent a few minutes at breakfast— we found the thing still following steadily in our wake. The children had in great measure gotten over their fear and had begun to crouch down and then suddenly rise up, opening their mouths at the thing, and cry out at it. Noticing that the creature did not react to their antics, they grew bolder and began screaming louder until they all shrieked shrilly. Suddenly, the hideous creature seemed roused by these cries, it raised its head in the air, uttered a strange bellow, and came forward at a great pace toward the ship. None of us could at first move from fear; the thing seemed to have grown in size, its eyeballs were burning more brightly; the children fell on the deck crying, and some of the women fainted. But those of us who remained standing, though still suffering from intense terror, still could not move.

It came swiftly up to the ship, always uttering the same peculiar cry or bellow. When but a few feet from the stern it suddenly turned and came up close on the port side. Here the side awnings had been put up to keep off the sun, but three of us rushed up to the awning and quickly tore it down so that we could better watch the creature. I must say that while doing this I was still suffering from extreme fear, but my curiosity was so irresistible that I could only act as I did. No sooner was the thing level with us than it raised itself with a sudden movement high out of the water, till its head was thirty or forty feet above us. It still uttered the same peculiar bellow. Under our intense curiosity we stood out on the bulwarks to follow its movement. It opened a great mouth, cried more loudly than before, and made three blows at the mainmast. The last of these touched it, and caused the ship to sway violently, so that we were nearly cast off into the water. When we looked again for the thing, it had disappeared. There was no ripple, no disturbance of any kind in the water. We constantly looked for it during the rest of that day, but it never appeared again.

After lunch was finished, the captain rose and asked us all to remain for a few minutes. He shortly referred to the strange sight we had seen that day, laying down the fact that he himself had not seen it, and he went on: "Now none of you can doubt what you saw; but I advise you not to talk about it. That was the sea serpent you saw. But again, I would not talk about it. It only leads to making people laugh and the papers take the story and joke about it. It won't do you any good. The late Captain Parish spoke of it and that captain never got over it— never. Remember, though, I saw *nothing*!"

3

An Errand at Midnight

On the east bank of the Red River, opposite the town of Alexandria, lies a long stretch of pine barrens, which extends a great many miles. On the western bank of the river the soil is as fertile, or more so, than the rich lands of the Mississippi Valley, so of course no attention is paid to the poor sandy soil of the Fine Hills. Yet to a certain extent these were utilized by the wealthy planters, who built their summer residences here before the civil war and spent three months out of the twelve where they could enjoy the pure fresh air and delicious spring water of the Pine Hills.

Mr. Layton, an impoverished planter, had found himself compelled to make a permanent home of this pine woods refuge. There he and his two children, James, a boy of twelve, and Elsie, a girl of two years younger, lived, with no neighbors nearer than three miles. About four miles from Mr. Layton's place was the little village of Pineville.

To a planter accustomed to rich lands and heavy crops, the meager sandy hills were a battle. But Mr. Layton brought some scientific knowledge to his farming, and despite its natural poverty, wrested some very fair crops of corn and cotton from his pine lands. Then his two motherless children were healthy and happy, for they remembered no other home. James was his father's assistant, and Elsie, despite her extreme youth, was almost as helpful and useful as if she had been twenty instead of ten.

Such a thoughtful little woman as she was! Very pretty, too, with black eyes and yellow hair, and a certain odd preciseness of speech, which grew out of her lonely life with books, which were her usual companions. It was a clear, bright September evening. Elsie sat in the broad gallery in front of the house, sewing, and watching her father, who was driving his wagon through the lane with the last load of corn.

"Have supper ready before dark, Elsie," he called out to her. "I've sent James ten miles off on business, and he'll not get back until tomorrow. I'll have to work after supper to get all this corn in, but it will be until midnight, so it don't matter much."

Elsie put up her sewing, and before dusk supper was on the table. Her father ate hastily but stopped as he went out to kiss her.

"You are the best little daughter in the world," he said, "and what would papa do without his Elsie? Don't sit up for me, dear, for I may be late tonight."

To go to bed without a final goodnight to her father was impossible for the little girl. She had her lessons to study, and a new Youth's Companion to read, and Elsie, like many other children in Louisiana, thought the little paper was the nicest in the world. So, she read on, every now and then stopping to listen to the thud of the corn as her father threw it up in the barn, and to his cheery whistle.

"Isn't it a pity papa hasn't anyone to help him?" She thought. "Tom went to see his wife" (Tom was a hired man), "and James is away too, and poor papa won't get finished for hours."

What farther thoughts passed through the child's mind were suddenly ended by a terrible crash and a loud cry from the barn, which was but a short distance from the house. Elsie sprung to her feet; her heart full of terror. She flew, rather than ran, to the barn, but before she reached it she heard her father's groans, and found him lying on the ground.

"I fell from the loft," he gasped. "I'm terribly hurt in my leg and side. I can't seem to move."

"Oh, papa, Mammy Martha and I can help you to the house." Elsie tried to restrain her sobs. Mammy Martha had nursed her father since his infancy. She served as a grandmotherly figure to the Layton family ever since. A former slave, the woman has had a long and eventful life.

"Call her," he said, faintly.

But Mammy Martha had heard the fall as well as Elsie and came hobbling up as fast as her rheumatic limbs would let her.

"Oh, my," she cried out, "what you gone and done, honey? Fell from the loft, eh? Oh, Mars Walter, is you never goin' to stop cavortin' round and climbin' as if you was young? What's hurt the most, honey?"

"Don't stop to look now. Try and get me in the house," he said.

Elsie was terrified at her father's ghastly face, plainly visible in the moonlight, and his faint voice. It was an agonizing journey over the few hundred yards between the barn and the house. With the assistance of the woman and the child, Mr. Layton pushed himself along, though the excruciating pain would compel constant pauses. To Elsie, it seemed as if hours must have elapsed before her father was dragged into a sitting room on the ground floor, for he could not be lifted up the steps to his bedroom. As they placed pillows around and underneath him, he fainted away.

"Don't scream, honey," said the old woman, who knelt down to examine his injuries, "he ain't dead; he's only passed out from the pain. He's mighty bad hurt, though, and I fear his leg is broke. Oh, child, if we don't get a doctor to him right away, he'll die for sure. What we gonna to do since James and Tom is away? And it's almost midnight at that." She wrung her hands in the extremity of despair.

As the old woman spoke, Elsie had seized a shawl and wrapped herself in it. "I'm going for Dr. Wilson, mammy," she said.

"You'd go four miles through de woods by your lone self? You'se crazy for sure."

"I'm going," she said, moving to the door with a white, determined face. "I'm not afraid, and when papa asks for me, don't tell him where I've gone."

In a moment she was out of the house and running down the lane. She paused for one minute to see if any horse was in the lot that she might ride, but the bars were down and the lot empty. Elsie was a fearless child, and every step of the way to Pineville was as familiar to her as her own yard. On she sped, through dark thickets and open spaces, where the tall, whispering pines made scarce any shadow; over shallow, pebbly-bottomed creeks; her little feet never pausing, and the little innocent heart knowing no thrill of fear save for the father she was speeding to save.

Three miles were accomplished, and she passed a large house some distance from the road— the Hill Farm, where her two friends, Rose and Jennie, lived. There was a light still burning in one of the rooms. A sod rose in Elsie's throat.

"Little do they think who is passing by now," she thought, "and what a dreadful thing has happened." Another mile, and she was knocking at Dr. Wilson's door, who, fortunately for her, had just returned from a professional visit, and whose horse, unsaddled, stood at the door.

"Elsie Layton!" cried the astonished doctor, who answered her summons. "Child, what are you doing at this time of night, alone and on foot, too? What's the matter?"

Her story was soon told to two sympathizing listeners, for Mrs. Wilson had joined her husband at the door.

"Fortunately, my horse hasn't been unsaddled," said the doctor. "Go in with Mrs. Wilson, child, and she will give you a cup of tea, and then we'll start. You can ride behind me."

No. Elsie wanted no tea. She wanted nothing but to be off and on the way home. Prince, the doctor's horse, had never carried double and he wasn't going to begin for Elsie or anybody else. He reared and backed and pranced in such an alarming manner that Elsie had to slip off as best she could.

"No use trying," said the doctor. "Prince has made up his

mind that he won't take you. Stay with Mrs. Wilson tonight, my dear, and rest assured I will not leave your father." He put spurs to his horse and was off like a flash.

"Yes, come in, Elsie," said Mrs. Wilson kindly. "You know you can start back at daylight in the morning, if you choose."

For the first time that evening Elsie broke down utterly and burst into a passion of tears and sobs. "I can't stay," she cried. "I would die if I had to stay away from papa tonight. I made it this far on foot. I'm not afraid; I'm not tired. Oh, Mrs. Wilson, I must go!"

And go she did, despite the good lady's pleas and even anger. "I suppose there is really, no danger," Mrs. Wilson thought, "but to think of that little creature being in the woods at this hour."

Elsie herself now that she had gained her point, had pretty much the same thoughts. The moon was going down, and the shadows lay black on the hillsides. Fatigue was beginning to tell upon her, now that the strain was relaxed, and her heart throbbed wildly whenever a sudden sound broke upon the stillness of the night. She was not far from the village when the noise of voices and of horses' feet on the road behind her caused her an involuntary panic, which she could not account for herself at the time.

She stepped into a thick cluster of bushes, and crouching among them, waiting for the riders to pass. Just as they reached her hiding place one of the men (there were two of them) stopped his horse and dismounted.

"It's this rotten girth again," he said. "Hand me your knife."

Elsie saw his face in the waning light and recognized it immediately. It was Dick Simmons, a noted ruffian, who had fled the country six months before for crimes that he had committed, and whom no one in that parish ever expected to see again. The other was another man whom she didn't recognize.

"Now, Bill, you are sure what you tell me?" Bill Lyons, she remembered, was a blacksmith employed on the Hill Farm.

"Course I am," Bill answered, "I was standin' on the gallery by the parlor door, when Hill come from Harrisonburg, where he had been sellin' a lot of cattle. I was fixin' the lock, and he never seen me. I seen him put the money in the top drawer of the desk, and he said to the ole ooman: 'Sally, I feared to keep all this money in the house tonight, but it's too late to go to town.'"

"Very well; I'm goin' on your word and if you've lied, you know how I settle with folks, don't you? Now do you remember all you've gotta do?"

"Yes, I got the kerosene and the matches. We're to set the barn ablaze and when the folks run out we break in to the drawer and take the money."

"I'll be bound you remember that," said the ruffian with a hoarse laugh. "Is the parlor locked?"

"If it is, here's a key," and he held something up.

"Very well. Now for my mask. I've got an account to settle with the old man at the farm, for he's been persecutin' me, and I reckon he'll lose some money tonight, and something else, too, if he don't keep out of my way."

The man mounted his horse. Shaking with every limb, Elsie watched them ride slowly down the road. What could be done to save her friends from the evil fate which was creeping upon them? Like a flash she remembered an unused path which cuts off more than half a mile from the main road. She could not be far from the path, which led directly to Mr. Hill's backyard; in fact, it was one made by the little girls and herself on their tree nut expeditions.

The men were moving slowly down the road. She could strike across and get to the farm before them. The little tired feet grew fleet when she thought of this. Yes, here is the turning, for dark as it was getting, the starlight showed her the hickory tree which stood where the path entered the road. She plunged into it, the briers tearing her at every step. But she felt nothing, heeded nothing, until she stood beneath the window of Mrs. Hill's bedroom. The dog had growled at her, but at the sound of her well-known voice had grown quiet again. She knocked at the window.

"Who is that?" called out Mr. Hill, startled from his sleep.

"It's me Elsie Layton. Don't make a noise, but let me in."

"Elsie!" cried the astonished couple, opening the door; the little girl staggered in, and for a moment thought she would faint, so utterly exhausted and overcome was she. But there was much to be told, and as soon as Mr. Hill understood the peril before him, he called his son and, posting him in the room where the money was deposited, hastened himself to the barn.

"Don't be scared," he said as he went out, "if you hear a shot or two. I'll have the advantage of the rascals, for they won't expect me, and I shall be looking for them. Willis, too, is well armed, and I reckon two are enough to deal with such fellows."

Nearly a quarter of an hour passes, and the dog barked

furiously, but suddenly ceased. "He knows Bill," whispered Mrs. Hill, "that's silenced him."

The light had been put out in the house, and the watchers sat silent and expectant. Then came a shot at the barn, and another loud bang, and Mr. Hill's voice shouting: "I've got one of 'em. The other is running as fast as his legs will carry him down the road."

In a few minutes Mr. Hill was back at the house. "I haven't killed the scamp. I only intended to wound him, so as to prevent him doing mischief. It's Dick Simmons, and I've secured him so that he will be safe until the authorities can take him to town. Now, wife, I need a mattress and some linen. If the fellow is a scamp, he must be treated humanely."

Now that the excitement was over, Elsie's thoughts returned to her father. "Oh, I must go!" She cried. "I was afraid while those men were on the road. Goodnight, all."

Mr. Hill laid his hand on her shoulder. "Going to trot back on those tired little feet of yours, eh, and past midnight? Willis, harness up the buggy right off, and take Elsie home; and he can bring the doctor back with him, if he's not needed by your father. I haven't thanked you, little girl, though you've saved my property, and possibly my life, too. But I'll never forget it, and possibly I may be able to do you a good turn before long. I'm proud of you, my child, and your father is a happy man to have such a daughter."

Speeding along in the buggy, the night seemed a fever dream to little Elsie. Would she ever forget it, or would her heart ever cease beating so strangely? It was a dream, however, which had a happy ending, for when she reached home and entered her father's room to the utter astonishment of Dr. Wilson, who thought her safe in Pineville, she found matters going well.

Her father was sound asleep, and not as seriously hurt as he had thought, although his leg was fractured. So little Elsie got ready for bed with a heart full of thankfulness. She will probably never forget the terrors of her midnight walk, but then she will also remember the good it accomplished.

4

Aunt Eliza's Ghost Story

The clock had struck eleven. We were still sitting on the hearthrug, over the remains of the wood fire that had sparkled and crackled in the huge old fireplace, filling the room with its light and warmth, now reduced to a few bright coals, casting occasional glimmerings of fitful light over the low ceiling of the spacious room. We had begun our "ante-bed" talk, under the influence of the bright fire. Under the influence of the dying fire, our conversation became more restrained and sober. There was a slight tap at the door, which startled us, and Aunt Eliza's bright face peeped in.

"Why, girls, not in bed yet?"

"Oh, Aunt Eliza," we exclaimed, "come and tell us a ghost story." She came in and took her seat on the rug in our midst.

"I can't tell a ghost story," she said, "but I will tell you what happened to me once, and you can call it what you please—but it is true, perfectly true."

We all know Aunt Eliza; no truer woman, in every sense of the word, lived than she, and we know hers to be a true tale if she says so.

"Well," she began boldly at first, but with an earnest tremulousness in her voice as she progressed that showed time had not obliterated traces of the excitement her experience must have produced in her at the moment, "some twelve years ago, your uncle had a little controversy about some land, in a certain county on the Mississippi River, which, after much delay, it was agreed by the parties, should be settled by arbitration. The care compelled your uncle to spend some weeks in Grenada, the county seat of the county where the land lay. Ever since our marriage I had kept your uncle's papers and accounts for him, for he was the most careless man in his business. So, he insisted I could be of service to him in Grenada, in preparing and classifying his memorandum for the hands of the arbitrator.

"Well, to make my story short, I went with him, leaving the house and the children and the farm hands to care for themselves and each other. The day before I left, I rode into town to see Mrs. Dalton, an intimate friend, to tell her of my going, and to ask her to come over to the farmhouse once in a while, and 'have an eye on things' there, which she readily promised to do.

"I stayed a whole week in Granada, in a miserable, dirty tavern, making memorandum and copying testimony, and helping all I could to get order out of the chaos of an old, unsettled, badly managed partnership. Saturday night I laid down on the hard tavern bed, pretty worn out with the kind of work distasteful to most women, doubly so for me.

"Early Sunday morning— it was scarcely light that short December day— I awoke with an undeniable urge to go home right away on the first boat. I could listen to no persuasion from your uncle. I felt like something was going amiss at home.

"So, about ten o'clock, a large boat stopped at Grenada, on her downward trip. The clerk, a hunchback, came ashore to receive some freight. Your uncle put me under his charge, and we were soon off. There were only a few passengers and I sat alone all day; so, as night drew near, I felt exceedingly nervous and anxious. One by one the passengers dropped off, until I was left the sole occupant of the long dreary looking saloon. A cabin boy passed along, silently extinguishing all the lights except one burner in each chandelier. I knew I would reach home about midnight, so there was no use in going to bed even if I could have slept. On one table was a Bible; I opened it, and vainly tried to read. The light was dim, and, besides, I could not concentrate my thoughts.

"I closed the book and looked up and down. There was not a soul visible in the long cabin of that boat, which seemed to me then, and seems to me now, the longest boat ride I was ever on. At the extreme bow end was a piano between the two doors that opened upon the guards, or the back way, I never knew which. There was a Frank Leslie book, or something of that sort, a pictorial, lying upon the sofa. I tried to look at the pictures, and I mechanically tuned the pages, but I literally saw nothing.

"At last, as a last resort— I couldn't sit still, I couldn't read, I couldn't sleep— I got up and walked the cabin come distance up and down, and up again, when, behold standing in the doorway, on the left of the piano, was Mrs. Dalton, the same light dress upon her she wore the day we departed, the same sweetly sad smile upon her face, and, with extended hand, as though to greet me. I was perhaps twenty feet off, but my eyes riveted upon her. I quickened my step, my eyes brightened, my lips were forming words of affection. I put forth my hand and touched her. A thrill went through me like what would have been felt by a sudden contact with cold, burnished brass. My hand touched the bolt of the door— the door was closed shut— the cabin was empty.

"I heard my own heartbeat like a drum, as I sank, appalled, upon the sofa. A voice roused me: 'Is anything the matter with you, madam?'

"It was the voice of the hunchback clerk.

'I have been watching you some minutes from my office window; you seem painfully nervous.'

"I could only answer that I was in fact nervous. So, he sat by me, trying to interest me— talking, talking; I never had the remotest idea what the poor man was saying. His voice was still droning in my ears when the sudden whistle of the boat announced my proximity to home. The whistle and the bell made a fearful ding. It was past two o'clock, the witching hour, when the boat landed in front of our home. The carriage driver, John, was seen coming rapidly down from the house with a lantern.

"I could not wait for the boat to be made secure, or the plank run out, or hardly for John to get within reach of any voice.

"'All well at home, John?'"

"'All well, missus,' rung out the man's cheery voice, as we walked up to the house, John and I, all alone.

"'And the children, John?'"

"'All well, missus.'"

"'And Mrs. Dalton, John?' I found courage to say.

"'Oh, Lord! Missus, Mrs. Dalton died yesterday morning.'"

"'Oh John!' I cried.

"'Yes, missus; it was awful sudden. She had a stroke at the dinner table Saturday and never recovered. She died peaceful like on Sunday.'"

Aunt Eliza rose with the words of the faithful servant upon her lips, kissed us all silently, and vanished from the room. The last glimmering of light had disappeared from the coals and from the hearth full of ashes, and so we girls crept silently to bed.

5

━━━

The Suicide of the Pont Neuf

At four o'clock on the morning of October 23, 1833, Henry Cabrion, a young journalist, who resided at the Hotel de l'Odeon, near the School of Medicine in the Latin quarter of Paris, returned home from drinking on the Boulevards, by the way of the Pont Neuf. It was a dismal, foggy morning, damp and chill, and few people were abroad.

As Cabrion reached the middle of the bridge, he noted by the light of the waning oil-lamps which sparsely illuminated the roadway, a figure leaning against the railing in the shadow of one of the little sentry boxes which are posted over every pier of the bridge. It was the figure of a woman in a ball dress and without shawl, headdress, or other protection from the inclement weather.

In utter amazement at this singular appearance, the young

man paused and was about to cross the bridge and speak to the stranger, whom he supposed was perhaps homeless or unfortunate woman, when, with a sudden spring, the woman leaped upon the rail and with a shrill scream, plunged into the water below.

The tide was on the ebb and flowed swiftly through the arches of the bridge. In a moment, Cabrion could distinguish by the dim light of early morning a dark figure drifting from under the gloomy arch and floating past the barges of the city laundry workers which as that time congregated about the Pont Neuf.

As quickly as we could, the young man threw off his jacket upon the bridge, kicked off his boots and dropped from the parapet into the water. For a moment, the icy flood took away his breath, but he quickly recovered and struck out in the direction the body had drifted. He found it within a hundred yards of the bridge, lodged between two barges and clinging to the rudder gear of one with its lifeless hand.

Cabrion's calls for help soon summoned one of the boatmen from the cabin of the barge and the rescuer and rescued were dragged aboard. The warmth of the cabin and the combined efforts of the Cabrion and the boatman were able to revive the would-be suicide's heart. Little by little her breathing became regular and she opened her eyes.

"Where am I," she asked. "How did I come here?"

"By accident, Mademoiselle," returned Cabrion. "Do not disturb yourself. I will explain as soon as we can reach some place where you can be more comfortable."

The woman stared at him fixedly but made no reply and

suffered herself to be assisted to a cab which the boatman had summoned. By Cabrion's order the cab proceeded to his hotel, where a room was secured for the stranger. Within two hours, the unfortunate woman succumbed to pneumonia and fell into a raging fever.

In her fevered ravings, during which she was watched by Cabrion and the porter's wife of the house, the sick girl spoke frequently of someone named Langlaume, who seemed to have inflicted a great wrong upon her; but never by accident revealed her own name.

On the second day after her rescue, Cabrion sent a letter to the office of the Petite Journal, where he was employed, to make excuses for his absence. While lounging in the editorial rooms, he picked up a copy of the paper of the day. Among the first extracts upon which his eyes fell, read, "Murder!"

"On the morning of October 23, M. Etienne Langlaume, the wealthy stockholder, and proprietor of the Cafe Grenier, in the Place Vendome, was found extended upon a sofa in his drawing room, dead. He had been shot with one of his own guns, which had been taken from a little armory of curious weapons which he collected. No trace of his murderer has been discovered. The dead gentleman had evidently been shot while asleep and his countenance exhibited no signs of pain."

Cabrion read and re-read these lines in a sort of mental stupor. When he recovered his self-possession, however, he became determined to get to the bottom of this story. The next day, his patient was much better and the physician who was in attendance declared her out of danger. Within a week, she was so far recovered that Cabrion resolved at once to satisfy his doubts. He asked her the favor of a private interview. The request was granted, and he found his patient propped up with pillows seated at the window.

"I am happy that you have come, Monsieur," she said. "How can I ever thank you for your great kindness?"

"I do not desire thanks at all, Mademoiselle. My best reward is in seeing you recovered."

"I am recovered in body. But in mind…"

"In mind?"

The woman stared; her pale face crimsoned under the searching glance he bent upon her. As she made no reply he went on:

"Do you know anything of this, Mademoiselle?" he asked, at the same time handing her the extract from the Petite Journal, which he had clipped and preserved for the purpose.

"How should I know anything of it?" she faltered, after a hasty glance at the clipping. "What right have you to ask me such a question?"

"From what you spoke during your illness, I fancied you might be able to explain it— that is all."

The girl stared violently, and her entire manner changed at once.

"My God!" she cried, burying her face in her hands, "have I betrayed myself after all?"

Cabrion made no reply and allowed her passion to spend itself in silence. At last she spoke, nervously and with an accent of intense adjuration.

"I see, Monsieur, that you know all; but I beg and pray you to listen to my side of the story before judging me. You who have risked your life to save mine, and who has treated me with such generous kindness, will not surely turn your back upon a poor weak woman without lending her your ear?"

"Certainly not."

"What I am about to tell you is, I assure you, the truth in every detail. I am the murderess of Etinenne Langlaume."

"I thought so."

"My name is Charlotte Couchois. I was a milliner and lived at No. 15 Rue de Temple, where Langlaume first met me at a ball at Sceaux. He offered me money, professed love, and promised to marry me. What followed afterward you may guess. Three months ago, my child… his child… was born."

The speaker laid her face in her hands for a moment and then went on.

"Up to the birth of the child we lived together four days out of the seven. The others, he alleged, were spent on business in the country. After the child was born, he disappeared, leaving me destitute and in debt. So much so that I was compelled to resort to the streets for food for myself and comforts for my child.

"Last month the child fell ill, and I went in search of its father to obtain money for medicine for it. I did not find him until the night of the 20th of October, when I met him going into a house in the Rue de Rivoli with a lady. I asked the porter who they were, and he told me M. Langlaume, the great restaurateur and his wife. His wife! I staggered away sick and faint. Badly as he had treated me, I had loved him until now— but now!

"I returned home to find my baby dead. I had not sufficient money to bury him and as a last resort went to the Rue du Rivoli and demanded to see M. Langlaume. He denied ever having known me, defied my threat to expose him to his wife and ordered me out of his house.

"That night I met a rich Prussian at the Mabille, who gave me sufficient money to bury my poor dead baby. The next night I met the Prussian again and we drank and rioted, as if my heart had been anything but the lump of lead it was and my thoughts anywhere but with the poor little grave in the gloomy cemetery under the cold rain. At midnight, we parted. He drove to a gaming house on the Boulevard, and I went home.

"My way led me through the Rue de Rivoli and as I passed his house a grim idea took possession of my maddened brain. I caused the carriage to stop, dismissed the coachman and returned to the house where the monster who had ruined me dwelt. I had no trouble in passing the porter, who recollected me from the day prior and probably fancied me some new mistress of his employer. I was soon in the room where I had parted with Langlaume yesterday.

"He had evidently spent the evening abroad, for he was lying on the lounge, fully dressed, and breathing heavily like a drunken man. What followed is very indistinct to me. I remember noting the glimmer of weapons in a cabinet in one corner of the room. My next recollection is of standing with a smoking gun in my hand and the smell of gunpowder in my nostrils. The sound of the weapon had deafened me but had not arouse him. He lay just as he had when I entered. He must have been instantly killed!"

"This is my story," Charlotte Cauchois resumed as a pause. "What followed you know better than I. I have concealed nothing from you and care not what use you may make of the knowledge. You can imagine from what you saw of me a few days ago that life is not of much value to me."

Cabrion rose with a respectful bow.

"You have nothing to fear from me, Madam," he said. "I have two thousand francs which are entirely as your service and a passport which was made out two weeks ago for my sister, who expected to leave Paris for a business visit to Germany. She is too ill to travel. It would be a pity that the passport should be wasted, especially as a train leaved at ten o'clock tonight."

After dark that evening, a carriage drove up to the door of the Hotel de l'Odeon and received a gentlemen and lady, closely veiled, who drove to the terminus of the Northwest-ern Railroad at Neuilly. Few words passed between them. The gentlemen purchased a ticket for Kehl and installed his companion in a first-class train car. As the whistle sounded for departure, he put his hand up to the window and bade her farewell.

"Adieu, Monsieur. How can I ever thank you, generous, noble heart."

"By not thanking me at all. You served the rascal right."

With a rush the train was off, and Cabrion turned away. Two days later he was arrested for assisting a felon to escape for the murder had been traced to Charlotte Cauchois. He made no effort to conceal his guilt, but told the story of the woman as she, now safe across the border, had told it to him. The Judge was interested, and the jury so moved that they returned a verdict of "not guilty" without leaving their seats. As Cabrion left the courtroom, he was met by two of the Judges who shook him by the hand.

The case was an orthodox nine day wonder in Paris, and Cabrion was for that time a celebrity. His salary on the paper was doubled and he gained the entree of more than one great mansion. Of Charlotte Cauchois he never heard again.

6

Life and Fortune Lost on the Race Course

In the latter part of the year 1866, Florence Paget became engaged to the Marquis of Hastings. The young Marquis was a debauchee of the weakest type. His father, the old Marquis, had died while his heir was low down in the years of his youth, leaving an estate reputed to be worth about £40,000 per annul, or $200,000 in gold. During the six or seven of his youth of the young Marquis, the income of the estate had been carefully husbanded by the trustees appointed under the will of his father, and when he came of age in 1865, despite the princely allowance given him during his collegiate course, there was still an apparent balance of savings to his credit of something over £200,000.

Unfortunately, however, for this young nobleman, he made, while at the university, the acquaintance of one of those sharks of civilized life, who, in the inscrutable wisdom of Providence, are permitted to exist. This man's name was Padwick, nominally a London lawyer, really a moneylender of the type whom Thackeray has portrayed in the character of Sherrick, in "Pendennis." Padwick loved profit and did not care how it was made, provided he was always on the "safe" side of the law. Young Hastings loved sport and did not care when or at what exorbitant rate of interest he obtained the money to pay for it. Padwick had no difficulty in supplying the means for the simple young Marquis to gratify his tastes— and his tastes, besides the taste for horse-racing, also ran to opera dancers and prima donna. The only thing that Padwick wanted was the signature of the Marquis and a certain three or four hundred per cent, interest, and whatever money he required was forthcoming.

A royal time the young man held at Oxford, and an equally royal bill he had to pay when he came from Alma Mater with an "honorary degree," a degree which is given to peers and the sons of peers, and which is called "honorary" to distinguish it from the "honorable" degree that is won by hard study.

When the young noble came of age, his accounts were settled by the clerks and accountants of the amiable Padwick, and it was found that not only had the reserve of £200,000 disappeared, but the annual rent-roll of £40,000 was some-what "dipped," as the English phrase it. In other words, the prodigal had spent the savings and Padwick held further obligations on the estate to a very considerable amount.

However, nothing daunted the young scapegrace, believing his resources still illimitable, started out on a new career of dissipation on the very night of the day on which he, in Westminster Abbey, was formally invested with the insignia of his rank and became, as he had been in name, the representative of the proud race who claimed their lineage from the first Earl who was ennobled by William of Normandy after the battle of Hastings in 1066. He had always been a lover of horses and horse racing and he vainly thought he could capture the blue ribbon of the Derby and, at the same time, replace the vast fortune he had spent in one single venture. His stable of thoroughbreds throughout his collegiate career had been a marvel amongst his fellow students if student isn't a misnomer under the circumstances. He had lavished vast sums of money on the purchase of unborn colts and had paid as high as ten thousand guineas for a yearling filly which came from the breeding stables of Sir Joseph Hawley, who, with "Blue Gown," had won the Derby, and, with "Blink Bonnie," both the Derby and the Oaks in 1865 and 1866. That ten thousand guinea speculation in 1877 proved the ruin of himself, his estate, and his life.

In the meantime, the young peer, as though his other follies had not been sufficient for one man, fell in love with Florence Paget, who was quite a few years older than him, and shared his love for the sport of horse racing. The Paget family, both in war and in social life, for two generations, had been known in the history of England for being reckless with their money or life. This Florence, with whom the luckless Marquis of Hastings became enamored, was, at the time, engaged to marry a Mr. Chaplin, a member of the firm Chaplin & Horne, which bears a similar relation the commerce of Britain like Wells Fargo & Co. did to the United States.

Chaplin was rich and a sportsman. He owned racehorses and ran them to win, and Chaplin had a trusted friend— a Capt. Machell, a retired officer of dragoons, who knew a little more about the management of horses and how to win with them than even Chaplin himself.

In December 1866, the flighty Florence Paget and Mr. Chaplin were to have been wedded, but just on the eve of the projected marriage, the night before it was to have been consummated, Florence bolted with her enamored Marquis by the Dover train to Paris, where they were married at the British Embassy the next day. Chaplin was naturally mad and sought revenge. The mare for which the Marquis had paid the thousand guineas for had won the Champagne stakes at Doncaster the September before, and she was a prominent favorite for the Derby, which was to be run the following May. Chaplin also had a horse entered for the same race, a horse named Hermit and Capt. Machell was superintending the training-ground in Yorkshire. Machell tried the horse thoroughly, but quietly, and came to certain conclusions concerning his running capacity, which was mentioned to only that of his friend Mr. Chaplin. The horse was believed by both men to be a good one and capable of winning, or at least "getting a place," if only that dangerous mare Lady Elizabeth were out of the way. And here, perhaps, it will be well to explain what is understood in English turf parlance as gets a place.

In all races where more than two or three horses run, the rule is for the second horse to obtain a share of the principal prize, while the third saves the money which its owner has had to pay at the time of entering it for the race. Thus, the three first horses are said to be "placed," or to "get a place," and a favorite mode of betting is to stake a certain sum of money on a horse to win, and another similar sum on his being placed. The general rule of the odds is that in backing a horse for a place only one-fourth the odds are given. That is to say, that if the current betting be eight to one against a particular horse winning, the odds against his being either first, second or third will be two to one.

Captain Machell and Mr. Chaplin, confident as they were in the prowess of their horse, were far too shrewd to show this confidence by openly putting their money up on him, and on the morning of the race he was still ranked as an "out-sider," forty to one being offered against him. The Marquis of Hastings, on the other hand, was not only certain that Lady Elizabeth would win, but backed her to win to an enormous amount, and continued his operations till on the day of the race he and the friends of the mare had to bet three to two on her winning in order to get any money on her. The wildest excitement that had ever been seen on any racecourse pre-vailed on that Wednesday in May 1867, which was to witness the total ruin of one of the finest fortunes in England.

The day was miserably wet and gloomy and the mud in the approaches of the course was ankle deep. But still, at least half a million people were out at Epson to see the race. The "Hill," the grandstand and fifty other stands were crowded with representatives of the fashion and beauty of England's capital, while along each side of the course from the famous Tottenham corner, stretched a double half mile of densely packed members of the lower stratum of English so-ciety. There were twenty-seven horses in the field and great difficulty was experienced in securing a fair start, no little of the difficulty being experienced by the vicious temper of the favorite, who had been groomed to perfection, and had been led from the saddling paddock amid a crowd of enthusiastic admirers, while Hermit was shaggy, unkempt and slovenly in appearance, somewhat undersized, and looking very little like a thoroughbred in a high condition of training. Finally, a fair start was obtained, and the hooves of twenty-seven of the choicest horses in England beat thunder out of the turf as they sped over Epsom Downs and disappeared in the bottom land beyond "The Hill." Soon the struggling mass of many-colored jockey jackets could be distinguished rising to view amid the gorse brush on the opposite side of the course. Telescopes and field-glasses were brought into requisition and the universal cry was, "Where is the Lady?" The answer was soon found; she was in the ruck in the rear— well up, but still in the rear.

"Ah," said her backers, "Fordham (the rider) knows what he is about," and a sigh of relief passed around, while the idea gained ground that he was saving the mare's strength for the straight rushing. But those hopes speedily died out; and when the turn was reached, at Tottenham corner, generally the deciding point for "a place" in all Derby races, the cry went up, "She's nowhere!" It proved to be so, for when the leading dozen horses passed the judge's stand the despised outsider, Hermit, was the first and Lady Elizabeth walked into the weighing paddock.

Then there was a scene which utterly baffles description. Curses both loud and deep rent the air and a throng of well-dressed men, and women too, crowded onto the turf and into the "ring," yelling their imprecations on everybody and everything that could by any possibility have been supposed to have brought about the disastrous result. The book-makers—all save one— looked serene, for this class of genres conduct their business on certain mathematically calculated plans and to them it does not amount to the value of a rush which side wins or loses. They hold the line under every possible circumstance and are serenely indifferent to facts which bring ruin and disgrace on thousands. The one exception was a certain Mr. Steele, who had the unfortunate Marquis name on his books for an enormous sum, and who, on settling day, which was the following Friday, posted the Marquis of Hastings as a defaulter. The total losses incurred by the noble noodle had been variously estimated from £100,000 to £120,000 sterling, and that, taken in connection with his already "dipped" revenue and known untrustworthy habits, ruined him.

On the Friday when he was posted, he was ordered out of the "ring," to which any plebeian can obtain admission on payment of a guinea, by Steel, the bookmaker, who had been a carpenter working for daily wages in Brighton and who had hardly sufficient education to write his own name. The disgrace, coupled with his dissipated habits, brought the foolish young Marquis to his grave and a few months later a quiet funeral, at which not half a dozen people were present, wound up the last of the direct line of one of the oldest families in the United Kingdom.

Chaplin, as before indicated, did not bet much on his horse— certainly he did not win more than was sufficient to pay the expenses of the race. But he had secured a deep and lasting revenge and won the highest honor of the turf at one stroke. He later became a member of Parliament and was looked upon as one of the most useful businessmen in the House.

Machell took a little care of himself on that day and invested about £1,000 ($5,000) in backing Hermit at odds of forty to one and consequently cleared some $200,000 by the day's end.

It was stated at the time that the reason why Lady Elizabeth broke down was well known to Captain Machell and that he had caused certain drugs, known to horsemen, to be administered to the mare on the night preceding the race; but these statements were never substantiated and in the absence of positive evidence should hardly be believed. But the fact remains, that the light conduct of one high-born woman was the immediate means of bringing about the ruin and death of the one of the proudest families in England.

7

Gideon Gadsby's Christmas

He was a very lonely man, this Gideon Gadsby, despite all his wealth. Years ago, he had married a woman much younger than himself. Had she lived, he might have been happier and better, but she had been dead twelve years and no other living person had filled her place in the merchant's heart. She had left only one child and despite his coldness he had lavished upon this little one a love only less strong than that he had borne her mother. At eighteen this girl had married against his will a poor clerk that he had taken into his employ. He had cast her off forever and now her name was never mentioned in his house. The refreshments by his side remained untouched and the merchant sat with his hands folded wearily and his eyes fixed absently on the fire— so still, so tranquil, that one might have thought him asleep. As he sat there, through the storm, and through the closed and curtained windows of the room, came the sweet tones of the midnight chimes of Trinity. The music of the bells filled the air, rising and falling with the wind. It was a glad and solemn song they sung, and it was a glad and solemn tale they told; for they sang that Christ was born.

"Gideon Gadsby!"

The voice was so soft and yet so distinct and sweet, that it thrilled the merchant to his soul. "Gideon Gadsby," the voice said, "are you glad that Christmas has come again?"

The voice came from the fire and the merchant glanced down at the hearth.

There, standing just before him was a strange but beautiful figure. It seemed like an angel, for its face was radiant with purity and beauty; and its garments were of spotless white.

"Listen to me," said the little figure, softly, "I am Conscience and I have come to speak with you. We have been strangers for a long time, but I have come back to you again. You must hear me tonight, for you cannot drive me away until morning; and O, if you are wise, Gideon Gadsby, do not drive me away!"

The merchant sat silent and trembling. He knew he was powerless and could not take his eyes from the little figure on the hearth. But it was little no longer, for it grew in size every moment, until it assumed a gigantic form and a face so stern and terrible that the merchant almost shrieked with terror as he gazed at it.

"What do you want with me?" he gasped.

"I will show you," said the figure, solemnly. "Come with me!"

The merchant felt a strong hand grasp him by the shoulder and the next moment he was borne through space and time with a speed so rapid that it deprived him of the ability to cry out. Suddenly there was a pause, and he opened his eyes. He stared in astonishment at the scene before him.

It was a small, plainly furnished room. Everything signified contentment, though at the same time an absence of riches. A woman, neither young nor old, sat by the fire and at her feet knelt a child, with his little hands folded in prayer. The merchant gazed at the scene in utter bewilderment. Then his eyes grew misty, and a great sob swelled up from his heart. He had recognized the two— the boy was himself, and the woman was his mother.

"It is a terrible thing, Gideon Gadsby," said the voice of Conscience, "for a parent to turn away a child."

The merchant shuddered. He was thinking of his own child and how he had turned from her plead for mercy. The figure laid its hand upon him and drew him away. He knew that they were now in New York again and that they were hurrying through the city amid the storm. The figure led him up long flights of stairs, until finally they entered a chamber so wretched that the merchant shrank in disgust. A flickering candle shed a feeble light through the room, adding to its misery a hundred-fold. On a low bed a man lay, pale and thin. A woman sat by the candle, sewing busily, her pale, thin face seeming even more ghastly by the uncertain light; and on a low pallet two children lay asleep— unconscious of the suffering around them. As he gazed the merchant saw that, despite the marks of care and suffering which it bore, the woman's face was wonderfully like that of his dead wife. No wonder, for the woman was his daughter. A cold sweat stood on his brow and his heart seemed to stop still.

Gideon Gadsby groaned and, turning to the figure, cried imploringly: "Let us leave this place! I cannot bear it."

The figure silently led him from the room and down the long stairs, out into the street again. It was no longer night there, for the sun was shining brightly and the thoroughfares were thronged with busy crowds hurrying to their destinations. The air was keen and frosty and the extra wrappings and comforters which the people wore, assured the merchant that it was very cold.

The figure led him into a large store on one of the business streets and only stopped when they reached the counting room, where several merchants were collected around the stove. Gideon Gadsby and his companion paused beside them, but the gentlemen did not seem conscious of their presence.

"What was that you said about Gideon Gadsby?" asked one.

"I said he is a heartless brute!" replied another.

"What has he done now?"

"He killed his daughter and her husband and children. They froze to death yesterday in a miserable hovel near East River. Think of it— on Christmas day, too— and old Gadsby rolling in wealth in his sumptuous home!"

Gideon's heart stood still.

"It is true," said the figure, solemnly. "In the sight of God, you have murdered your children."

Again, the merchant felt himself borne swiftly along and when he opened his eyes again, he found himself in his own home.

He stood in his chamber and involuntarily he marked the contrast between its luxurious comforts and the miserable garret in which his daughter had frozen to death. He saw, to his surprise, his desk, where he kept his private papers and a considerable sum of money, open, and one of his servants searching among the contents. He tried to spring forward to stop the man, but he could not move. When he endeavored to speak, his voice failed him. The figure pointed silently to the bed and Gideon looked helplessly in that direction.

A man lay on the bed, silent and motionless. His hands were clasped mutely on his breast and his eyes were wide open and staring blankly at the ceiling. Gideon bent over and gazed at the countenance, but he shrank back in horror and dismay. Never had he seen such a lock of despair as that dead man's face. So still, so terrible was it, that it seemed to be something supernatural. The merchant shrank back with a groan, for the face upon which he looked was his own.

"Is this to be the end?" he moaned.

"This will be the end," said the figure, solemnly. "To die alone, neglected, and unloved and without hope hereafter. God help you, Gideon Gadsby."

The figure slowly faded away and Gideon looked up with a start. He was sitting in his library, with the untasted refreshments on the stand by his side and the embers of the fireplace cold and lifeless in the grate before him. The gas was burning in the chandelier with a sickly glare and through the curtained windows, streamed and broad, full light of the Christmas sun. The merchant rubbed his eyes and stared around vacantly. Then his gaze rested on the portrait of his dead wife over the mantelpiece. The golden sunshine fell lovingly upon her face and the eyes of the woman who had been so dear to him seemed full of sweetness and tenderness as they shone down upon him, carrying light straight into his heart that had been so dark.

"O, God, be thanked! It is but a dream."

Another look into the dear eyes of the woman who had loved him, and he sank down on his knees and bowed his head slowly and reverently. Gideon Gadsby was praying. It was still early morning when the handsome carriage of the merchant drove by the park on its way to East River.

Down through the vile streets, reeking with filth and crime and misery, that mark the worst quarter of the great city, the splendid carriage passed. It paused before a miserable dwelling and the merchant sprang out with a flushed, excited face and hurried up the rickety stairs, fearing the one part of his dream might be true after all. He pushed open a door and entered the miserable room. A glance satisfied him that the blessed day had brought no joy to the occupants of this sad abode. A woman, pale and careworn, sat by an empty grate, with a look of hopelessness on her sweet, young face, while a man, gaunt and sickly, lay on the bed with closed eyes and two children rested on a rude pallet, still happy in their innocent slumbers.

Startled by the noise, the woman looked up. Gideon's eyes clouded and he held out his arms and faltered:

"My daughter, forgive me!"

With a glad cry she sprang into his arms and the penitent father felt that he was forgiven. The princely mansion had never seemed so cheery before as on this blessed Christmas when it rang with the merry shouts of the children and echoed the soft laughter of the elder ones; and as Gideon Gadsby listened, he lifted up his heart and blessed God for the dream He had sent him to bring back so much happiness.

8

The Photograph Mystery

The last object viewed in life is said to be so ingrained upon the retina of the eye that it can be photographed after death. When this theory was first broached, an occasional effort was made to test its accuracy as a means of identifying murders; and the most extraordinary of these cases forms the groundwork of the present story.

In the summer of 1863, a young physician named Edward Stone commenced practice in a certain village not far from New York City. In saying that he commenced practice, I mean that he seriously intended to do so when patients were forthcoming. In his medical studies he made a specialty of diseases of the eye; but as there is nothing of any account for an oculist in a small village, he made a virtue of necessity and put up his sign as physician merely. He invested all the money he had in the world in a cheap little cottage, which he selected, not for its business advantages, but because it was the very highest of perfection in all other respects. For the fact was, he was engaged to be married as soon as his circumstances would admit. His betrothed wife was Ella Thorne, the daughter of the village lawyer; and poor as Edward was, he would not have exchanged her silver voice for a golden dower.

When he first entered into possession, he only furnished the two lower rooms of the house, the front one being his consulting room and the rear one his bedroom. The visits of patients were like those of angels, "few and far between;" but whenever he had an extra run of luck, he and Ella would have a fine time shopping together, in order to furnish his office and have it ready when the auspicious moment arrived.

To keep up appearances— an indispensable thing in this world— the doctor was obliged to keep someone to answer the door and make himself generally useful. In accordance with an invariable custom, the doctor got the largest youth he could obtain for the money; and this happened to be a dogged fellow, who enjoyed the enviable reputation of having "a devil in him." Of course, the wages that Seth, as he was called, received from the doctor were not sufficient to keep body and soul together; and as he wrote an excellent hand, two birds were killed with one stone by Lawyer Thorne giving him occasional employment as copyist.

The summer passed by— autumn came and went— and even winter brought no improvement in Edward's prospects; and the poor fellow often wondered whether his flowering hopes would share the fate of everything else the summer had brought forth.

Just at this time, a wealthy man of science offered a large sum of money for the best treatise on the subject of optography. Being thoroughly conversant with everything pertaining to that subject, Edward Stone applied himself to the task like an enthusiast. He did not do this so much for the prize itself as for what lay behind it; for he saw a ruddy flame in his dingy fireplace and beside it sat Ella Thorne, with a child on her knee, as much like her as it is possible for any bud to be like a flower. Although it was but an imaginary flame, it lent a new sparkle to his eye, as he stays up night after night engaged in that labor of love. As the work progressed, he read it aloud to Ella and they laid a thousand foolish plans regarding the expenditure of the money— when he obtained it. So much was to be invested in the wedding dress; so much in a perfect rainbow of a carpet for the parlor, and, to cap the climax, Edward added, with an effort to be funny, "We will buy that gaudy picture of the Good Samaritan in Wellington boots and swallow-tailed coat, that we saw in the shop window the other day."

Neither Edward nor Ella entertained the possibility of a failure to secure the prize. But after the manuscript had been forwarded, they waited with their hearts in their mouths for the day upon which the successful competitor was to be announced. Every hawk they saw reconnoitering above the village seemed, to their anxious eyes, a carrier pigeon bearing the intelligence they so impatiently awaited. At length the momentous period arrived, and the result justified their most sanguine expectations. Edward was declared entitled to the prize and was duly notified to appear forthcoming and receive the amount in hard cash.

The two were almost beside themselves with joy, and the wedding day was set at once. Edward lost no time in securing the money, but, like most young doctors, he had no bank account; so, on returning home with the amount late at night, he took the precaution to fasten it in a belt along his waist. After dismissing Seth, who was waiting for his return, Edward sat down by his bedroom fire, and was soon lost in one of those reveries where everything is pink. Often when he sat beside Ella in church, the sun would suddenly strike through the painted window, and make the gloomy aisle burst into blossoms with rubies and emeralds; and thus, the enchanted vista of the future appeared to Edward Stone on that memorable night.

There was a brook just behind the cottage, but winter had laid its icy finger on its warbling lips— consequently the gurgling sound that broke the silence of midnight could not proceed from that. Whatever caused it, the gurgling sound soon ceased and was succeeded by the prolonged howl of a dog in the distance— that peculiar howl by which the superstitious know that someone is dying in the village.

The next morning, Seth was on his way to the cottage, as usual, when he encountered lawyer Thorne, who was just starting out for his morning walk.

"I think we are going to have a fine day," Thorne said to Seth.

"It may be," replied the latter; "but it will be a wintry one, if that red sky is any sign." The lawyer had an eye like a lynx, but for the life of him he could not discover the slightest tinge of red in the heavens.

"By the way," Thorne said, "as you have finished all but a

page or two of your last job, it will take you but a moment or two to do it now."

Seth was at first disinclined to comply; but he finally went in and sat down with pen in hand, waiting for the ink, which the lawyer brought from his desk in the adjoining room.

Before commencing, Seth drew his hand across his eyes, as if to brush away something which blurred his sight; and had scarcely written the first word before he started up and angrily exclaimed: "I didn't ask you for red ink!"

The ink was as black as the ace of spades; and this being Seth's second optical delusion that morning, the lawyer advised him to defer the copying for a short time. Seth then departed for the doctor's cottage and shortly afterward came rushing back to announce that he had found a hatchet embedded in Edward's skull. In consequence of his suspicious conduct at lawyer Stone's, Seth was promptly arrested, and was speedily brought to trial.

Directly after the murder, it transpired that the prize for the treatise was offered by a gentleman who knew of the terrible situation in which Edward Stone and Ella Thorne were in and by offering the prize, he accomplished the double purpose of advancing the interests of science and of rendering monetary assistance in a delicate way. Next to Ella herself, no one was so horrified by the murder as this gentleman; for, as it was followed by robbery, he reproached himself for being the indirect cause of the tragedy. In order to make all the amends in his power, he devoted all his energies to the prosecution of the suspected man. Being an enthusiast regarding the theory upon which poor Stone had written, he determined to reduce it into practice as a means of conviction. The gentleman employed one of the most skillful photographers in New York City to photograph the eye of the murdered man and thus obtain the portrait of the murderer.

On the day of the trial the photograph that was taken was brought into court in a sealed envelope; after the preliminary proof had been submitted, the photograph was duly exhibited to the jury. The foreman was a weather-beaten old man, who would have looked a wildcat in the eye with perfect composure; but he no sooner saw the photograph than he covered his face with his ruff hands and uttered a cry of horror that will echo in the ears of those that heard it until it is shut out by the coffin lid.

It was a photograph of Ella Thorne!

Everyone saw from the wild excitement that it would be useless to prosecute the matter further, and the prisoner was discharged from custody; of course, no one was so devoid of reason as to suspect Ella Thorne of any complicity in the crime. Years passed and the people of that village began to lose faith in the proverb that "murder will out," when Ella, who had devoted herself to deeds of charity since that awful period, was summoned to the bedside of Seth, who had been wounded in a drunken brawl. On her arrival, the drunken wretch spoke as follows, although some of the words gushed out with a mouthful of blood:

"There is not a creeping thing on God's earth that doesn't see the day it wished for wings; but nobody had the charity to suppose that I ever wanted to be any better than I was. Ever since I first saw you, I turned my back on God to worship the original of this portrait."

He fumbled under the bed for a moment, and she recoiled

in horror as he produced a miniature figure that looked exactly like Ella. She had given it to Edward Stone before his death and it was now smeared with his blood. Having exhibited this, Seth proceeded with his recital:

"Mine was a nature that could stand any number of kicks, when a single kind word would have been too much for me. But I didn't get it— so let that pass. Edward Stone was superior to me in everything but in love for you; when he came between us like a snake, I resolved to send him to the only place where I could meet him on equal terms. That place was the grave. A dying bed is no place for hypocrisy, and I admit that the money was one incentive to the murder; but when I saw him gazing at this miniature just as I struck him down, I drove the hatchet in an inch or two deeper as I thought of his love for you. I secreted that portrait with the money, and I want no other man to wear it next to his heart, as I often did at night when no curious eyes were about; so you are welcome to it. All the more so because it has the blood of Edward Stone upon it. I feel no remorse for what I did, although everything has looked red to me ever since his blood spurted up into my eyes and even those black clouds on yonder crimson sky look like vultures on a field of blood."

As he pointed upward, he fell back dead. The mystery connected with the photograph was solved; the face photographed from Edward's eye was the face of Ella's miniature an instant before it had closed forever.

9

Story of the Whale

Whaling was considered one of the most dangerous professions at the time in the 18th and 19th centuries. But the relations between officers and men were as brutal on the vessel in which Captain Davis sailed his first voyage as on most ships in other services. The captain and officers were tyrannical masters and the men vindictive slaves. The rope's end and, on one occasion the revolver, were the arguments used to bring refractory sinners to their senses. The officers swore at the men aloud and cheated them to their faces. The men swore at the officers under their breath and were treacherous in dark corners. Once there was a revolt and the men protected a lad from the captain's cat o' nine tails. The mutineers were imprisoned without trial by an ignorant consul of the United States in one of the Hawaiian ports and were released after many months by a war vessel. Quarrels, threats, blows, and desertions were a frequent occurrence and out of the large crew that sailed from New London, only four or five returned home in the same ship.

The good days of cooperation were waning when Captain Davis went to sea. But there was never a time when the crew refused to work or allowed a whale to pass without lowering the boats and cheerfully risking their lives in its capture; and a can of grog was never sent to the forecastle, nor a kind word said that did not awaken manifest gratitude in these poor sons of the sea. Considering all things, we think that the sailors were to be blamed least. A pathetic incident is related of the illness of a boy named Beers. He was left alone and unattended, without nourishment or medicines, on a narrow shelf in a foul smelling, vermin infested pantry. When one of the forecastle hands found him, he was deliriously murmuring the words repeatedly, "Oh, how lonely to die so far away from home and friends. How lonely, how lonely." When he recovered consciousness, he stroked the hand of his comrade and continued, "I should not mind dying near the shore in the track of other vessels; but here, so far at sea, how lonely, how lonely." His spirit was not released until after many hours of suffering and he died babbling of green fields.

All ills on board were treated with one formula. A powerful dose of Epsom salts was first administered to the patient and if that effected no improvement a still more powerful dose of a medicine called jalap followed, with the objective of neutralizing the salts. But if neither medicine produced a favorable change, they were supplemented by a potion of calomel that either killed or cured.

In the long voyage around Cape Horn to the sperm-whale

ground there are few incidents that have not been described before. The vessel is followed by the flying fish, the pilot fish, and the albatross and in smooth weather the crews put on drills to capture a dummy whale. A spar is towed astern and the greenhorns in the boats maneuver around it with a great deal of earnestness and are taught some of the tricks of the trade. As soon as they reach the banks of Brazil actual service is due and each man is alert for the stirring cry from the masthead, "There she blows!" The ship is under sail during the day only and in the night, she stands by under close reefed canvas, an arrangement which allows the crew long watches below and prepares them for hard toil during the day. The captain and mates strain their eyes across the waters and the humblest deck hand is not less zealous and anxious. When at first the word is heard from aloft and is repeated quick and often, the boats are manned with such alacrity and precision as is seldom seen elsewhere.

The American whale boats are unsurpassed in beauty, speed, and durability. They are twenty-eight feet long, swelling amidships to six feet in breadth. The gunwale is twenty-two inches above the keel amidships and rises with an accelerated curve to thirty-seven inches at each end. The elevation of bow and stern, and a clipper-like upper form, give them a duck-like capacity to ride advancing waves that would fill and sink ordinary boats. The boats can make ten miles an hour in a dead chase by oars alone.

The equipment of each consists of a line tub, in which are coiled 300 fathoms of the best hemp cord; a mast and spritsail; oars, harpoons, and lances; a small apparatus to extinguish the fires that might be ignited by the friction of the cord drawn from the reel; a water keg, lantern, candles, compass, waif flags on poles, and bandages for wounds. The harpoon is a barbed triangular iron, very sharp on the edges and the lance is a somewhat similar instrument.

In the boats that were described, the whales of the sea were chased and attacked. The animals were sometimes killed by the first dart of a harpoon and dies a quiet death; other times he or she fights for hours at a time, destroys boat after boat, mangles the men, and even charges at the ship itself. Such a giant that can strike with such ferocity was one of the first that Captain Davis had to encounter.

As soon as the harpoon had struck him the whale swiftly ran a short distance under water, carrying a line with him. Then turning in his course, he rose to the surface and rushed at full speed, with his head out of the water, for one of the boats which he stove in and rolled over. The captain's boat, in which Davis was bow oar, came to the rescue but as the captain saw that the men were not in immediate danger, and that a third boat was approaching, he left them swimming and attempted to coax the whale away from the wreck, which the enraged monster was threshing with his terrible jaw. Just then the whale noticed the swimmers and rushed toward them, with his jaw at right angles with his body. But before he could reach them, a second harpoon was hurled into him which accelerated his speed. He ran away to the windward, towing the captain's boat in his wake.

It was then the duty of the oarsman to grasp the fastening line and haul the boat alongside the whale so that the lance might be used upon the huge body. But it was impossible, owing to the increasing speed of the whale and the savage manner in which he tossed his flukes. The captain used an implement called a spade, with the hope of severing the tendons of his tail, and so bringing him to a halt; but the operation was unsuccessful, and he ran with undiminished speed, often rolling as he went, so as to give the flakes a side-cutting power, with the intention of crushing his little antagonist. Under similar circumstances the ordinary maneuver of the hunters is to sheer the boat to one side of the whale by taking a knotted loop of the line over one side of the boat.

In this instance, the oarsman had been tugging at the line for an hour but was utterly unable to get the boat in advance of the flukes of the whale. A little line might be gained for a short time, but it would soon be torn through the clinging hands, almost taking the flesh with it. This was certainly very aggravating to the excited captain. He was a little hard on his oarsmen and rather more than hinted at somebody's cowardice. With the aid of two others, he brought the boat right up to the side of the whale's body and tied a loop of the rope around one of the seats of the boat. The captain was delighted to be held up to his work so well and plied his lance thrust after thrust into the whale's side.

He would not spout blood and the little jets that came from the lance holes would not bleed a whale to death. The boat buried her nose in the waves and the bloody spray leaped over her sides as they swept onward. The majestic creature grew impatient at the captain's prodding. He turned across their course and the boat ran plump against his head.

"Slack line!" roared the captain. "Starn all, slack line, and starn!"

He turned in his tracks to step aft of the bow oarsman,

fearing the upward cut of the whale's jaw, when he saw that the line was fast to the thwart.

"For God's sake cut that line!" he shouted, as he sprang forward for the hatchet; but the loosened knot went over the side, as the whale came up under the forward part of the boat and carried the bow clear out of the water as he rounded slowly forward.

At this moment the captain and old Ben (the harpooner) occupied the stern of the boat and in the perilous moment the two old whalemen awaited the arrival of the oncoming strikes of the creature's tail. Fortunately, the blow was delayed a moment and when the thundering concussion came it missed the boat by a few feet. The other boats were out of sight and the ship's hull could be dimly seen on the horizon. For two hours more the whale ran and fought with redoubled energy. The captain got long darts with the lance but with no good effect. The iron drew and the victorious whale swam on.

It was nightfall when the worn-out crew reached the vessel and found that their comrades, whose boat had been wrecked, were all safe on board. The next day, the green but plucky bow oarsman was told that in fastening the line to the boat he had placed six men within an inch of death. If the whale had gone down, the frail craft and her crew would have been a quarter of a mile under water in less than a minute.

Numerous stories could be told of the heroic daring of whalemen and the prowess of the game which they seek. An infuriated whale is a vastly more terrible antagonist than the wildest and mightiest of land animals. His courage is equal to his power and instances are on record in which a sperm whale, after defeating the men in the boats, has rushed upon the ship, stove in her bow and sunk her. A boat or two lost is usually the smallest cost of an encounter, and often the crew are tossed high in the air by his monstrous flukes, with a bristling shower of harpoons, lances, and splinters following after. Coming to the water bruised and lacerated, the men are still pursued by the enemy and must avoid his jaws by diving under or crawling over him until one of the other boats has an opportunity to dispatch him. Whale ships do not carry surgeons, and the most horrible wounds are dressed unskillfully by the captain, who, in all probability, knows less of surgery than of Latin or Greek. Amputations are performed with carpenter's saws and other knives and wounds bandaged with canvas. If you should ever meet an old whaleman you may read in his patches and soars the evidence of the manifold perils of his profession.

In the pretty cemetery at Sag Harbor, Long Island, there is a marble monument bearing a touching record. It is in the form of a broken ship's mast with a rope twisted around the foot and engraved upon it are the names of six captains of whale ships belonging to the town, all of them under thirty years of age, who died, within ten years of each other, in an actual encounter with the monsters of the deep. An old whaleman who had escaped death several times used to declare that he only lived on borrowed time, a monument of God's infinite mercy.

10

A Vision of Hanging

Had Belcher, the Essex County, Ontario murderer, been executed on the 21st of December, as sentenced, it would have been his second execution. If this assertion reads strangely, I will do my best to explain it so that it reads perfectly plain.

Belcher was a calm man. He stained his hands with human blood only after he had brooded over his wrongs for weeks and only after he had concluded that his own life was a burden. He scarcely attempted a defense when his trial came on. He could have secured witnesses whose testimony would have influenced the jury in his favor, but he would not send for them. He could have made a statement excusing his crime in a measure and showing that he had been deeply wronged, but he would scarcely speak. When the Judge put on the black cap and sentenced Belcher to be hanged, the murderer exhibited less emotion than any other person in the court room. It was only after he had been ironed hand and foot and placed in the murderer's cell in the grim jail at Sandwich that he seemed to realize his situation.

"It's all right; I'll be there when wanted," he grimly observed, and he talked freely with the numerous journalists who bought interviews.

There were few residents of Essex County who wanted an execution to take place. The county has not had one for years; the influence of the anti-capital punishment people of Michigan is strongly felt along the border. Steps were soon taken to secure a commutation of sentence. Belcher was apathetic at first, being more inclined to put the noose over his head than to cast it from him. There came a reaction. Perhaps the winter sunshine pouring through the corridor warmed his heart at the same time. He could hear the merry shouts of the boys as they slid down the hill or skated on the river below and the musical jingle of the sleigh bells could not be kept out by the massive walls. Belcher wanted to live.

He wrenched at his irons with the strength of a giant and called out because the hours and days were flying so swiftly. He besought the press to plead his case; he called for lawyers; he remembered that he had witnesses. The strong man broke down and became a child, and every day, and every hour, outside of his sleep, he thought of the grim gallows, the fatal noose, and he saw himself dangling in the air. Three days before the reprieve came, he said he would die ready; but he said it with a face as white as snow and every nerve trembling with fear. Had he been taken to execution he could not have walked alone, and he would have sunk down on the trap. All Essex County was at last working in his favor. Petitions were circulated, mass meetings were held, and an irresistible influence was brought to bear on the Governor General.

Belcher hoped and feared. Reprieves are not so common in Canada that murderers in the shadow of the gallows can rely on them and keep their courage up. When Sheriff, and Warden, and the murderer were counting the hours, the reprieve came. Belcher escaped the gallows, but the doors of Kingston were to close on him for life. It was evening when the news came and when the telegram was read to him, he could not utter a word.

An hour before the sun went down, the jail was very quiet. It is always so when the shadow of death holds the key. Belcher paced up and down, his face haggard and worn and his eyes wearing such a look as one never sees outside the prison walls. Out in the courtyard men were at work, not at the gallows, but at some repairs. Belcher believed that the scaffold from which he was to swing was being erected and his heart must have stood still as he heard the hammer and saw the work. Leaning against the wall, his eyes fixed on vacancy, the murderer suffered all the pain that a real execution could inflict. Some of the prisoners were watching him. They saw him hold out his hands for the Sheriff to remove the irons. They saw him kneel in prayer. They saw him arise and look around as if following the officials to the gallows.

He looked up as if surveying the swaying noose, and a shudder passed over him. The prisoners could read his thoughts as plainly as if he had written them down. In imagination he mounted the gallows. He looked at the noose again and suddenly jerked his head aside, as if the rope had touched him. He bent his head as if to have it passed over and tightened around his neck.

When he stood as if waiting for the trap to spring, his face was no longer pale; it was so livid and distorted that almost every line of humanity was crushed out of sight. The trap fell, and with an awful gasp, a shout, a scream of agony, Belcher fell to the floor, his tongue protruding, his eyes open and glassy, and a froth oozing from his mouth. It was a quarter of an hour before he was fully resuscitated, and his first words were: "Oh, God how the rope cut into my neck!"

It was another fifteen minutes before the man could be convinced that his execution was imaginary. He had suffered all that a hangman's victim suffers, and in piteous tones he cried out, while the tears ran down his face "Don't hang me again! My throat in so sore!"

He had on a wool shirt, fitting loosely around his neck. They unbuttoned the collar, turned it down, and there was a bright red mark clear around the throat. Only facts are stated here, and people may theorize as they feel inclined. That mark did not go away for thirty hours, and the murderer complained of swollen tonsils and a sore throat. His reprieve came only after he had been hanged and yet it saved his life.

11

Judge and Executioner

About the beginning of November, in the year 1820, in the middle of the day, a sled drawn by a horse dashed through a small village in Russia and stopped in the courtyard of one of the largest houses. The horse had evidently run away and the sole occupant of the sled, a young woman, was lying motionless.

In less than a minute a great many of the villagers, who had been attracted by the clattering of the inhabitants of the house, roused by the appearance of the sled in the courtyard, surrounded the young woman. It was evident she was powerless to distinguish anyone around her. There was just a faint sign of life, and that was all; but to most of the bystanders, she looked far more dead than alive. She was carried into the house and restoratives were administered.

She had hardly recovered her consciousness, when questions of every sort and kind were put to her from all sides. She was asked who she was; where she came from; where she was going to; who was pursuing her, and how the horse had run away. The room in which she was placed was full of villagers, who had come in to satisfy their very natural curiosity.

Among the most excited of the questioners was a young serf about twenty years old, who held in his hand the hatchet with which he had been felling wood when the sled dashed through the quiet village. The beauty and painful grief of the woman seemed to have made rather an effect upon this young serf. He was certainly more anxious than the rest to hear her story, and was very prominent in his attentions, and put himself forward in endeavoring to offer her consolation.

At last, the object of all this excitement had so far recovered as to be enabled to yield to the entreaties of those who surrounded her, and in a broken voice and amid very general silence she spoke as follows:

"I had heard that an old relation of mine, who lives in a neighboring village, was dangerously ill, and I determined to set out and see if I could be of any assistance. Early this morning I harnessed our horse to the little sled and set out."

"Alone?" asked the young serf, pointedly, still swinging the hatchet in his hand.

The bystanders well understood the meaning of the question, and the same word seemed involuntarily to escape from their lips.

"Alone?"

It may be wise here to give a short explanation, which will account in some way for the surprise in the woman being alone. When the Russian troops had conquered Finland under the command of General Friedrich Wilhelm von

Buxhoeveden and were returning home again, they were followed by countless troops of bears and wolves, who raged and quarreled over the bodies of those who from time to time died of cold or fatigue and howled for the scraps of food left behind by the conquering army. The province which the army passed through was infested by fierce animals long after their departure, and they soon became the terror of the humble peasantry who lived in that district. They were not content with devouring the various domestic dogs and cats that came in their way, but fiercely attacked any human creature that crossed their path. It became impossible to travel in safety at any hour of the day upon even a frequented road without a very strong escort. Anyone who neglected these necessary precautions paid the penalty of his or her carelessness in a hideous death. In the course of the preceding winter, forty human beings in this particular district had fallen a prey either to wolves or bears.

"Alone!" answered the young woman in a strange, unnatural voice, half choked with sobs, "unhappily for me, I was not alone! Why, in heaven's name, did I risk such a journey? Don't compel me, I beg of you, to relate the horrors I have gone through, and all the miseries of that awful morning."

"What has happened to you? Who went with you?" still asked many of those who surrounded the woman, and whose attention and curiosity were now thoroughly roused.

"Miserable woman that I am," answered she, "I took with me my three little children, the oldest of whom was about five years old, the youngest a little darling only six months."

An exclamation of horror ran through the circle of bystanders, and each one at last seemed to guess the hideous truth. And then, amid a more awful silence than before, the young woman went on with her story.

"It was a lovely morning, the road in good order, and the old horse trotted merrily along. My two little boys played at my feet and the little one slept on my chest. I was in high spirits, and happy at the thought that I was able to get away, and so perhaps be of service to my poor old relative. My happiness, however, was not of very long duration. About an hour after our departure from the village, the thought struck me how daring and venturesome it was to travel alone with my little ones through a vast desert of snow, cut off from aid and, far away from any human habitation.

"Then for the first time I began to remember all the dreadful accidents that had befallen lonely travelers in our neighborhood, and almost made up my mind to turn back again. This fear grew upon me. and it increased more than ever when I perceived that the track in the snow had become so narrow that all chances of turning back in safety was cut off. I was obliged to go on, regardless of whether I wanted to or not. My terror kept increasing; but I dared not let the children know that I apprehended any danger; I listened anxiously and magnified the slightest sound I heard. The track got narrower and narrower until at last, as we were passing a little belt of fir trees, I heard distinctly behind me an awful sound. I knew well what it was in an instant, I turned around and saw that we were being pursued by a flock of hungry wolves. Now that the danger was so imminent, my courage began to get stronger.

"I madly lashed at the horse, and he set off at a wild and excited gallop. It was too late; two of the largest wolves, with red, glaring eyes and hideous open jaws, were already at the horse's flanks, and raced with him along the snow-covered track. On the horse's life depended on my life and that of my children. If he died, we were all lost. Cost what it might, the horse's life must be saved, I thought. A horrible thought flashed across me, and instead of repelling it I accepted it as an inspiration from heaven. In cold blood l made up my mind, and in cold blood I calculated the awful consequences of my plan. At this very instant my second boy, a child of three years old, clung to me and cried piteously. The boy's sobs seemed to excite the demonic animals more than ever, and they gained on the galloping horse.

"Without knowing what I was doing, and with, almost an involuntary movement, I seized the shrieking child by the hair and dropped him behind the sled. I saw him sink into the soft snow; there was one wild cry, and then the wolves stopped short where the boy had fallen. All this passed in less than an instant. For a minute I thought we were saved; but it was not so. The little one's cries had hardly died away in the distance when two more wolves appeared at the side of the sled, the awful sacrifice I had made had been useless, and we were in as much danger as ever. The same fiendish thought took possession of me, and again my mind was made up. I looked first to the little darling nestling closely to my breast and then I turned to my eldest by, who was pale with fear and clutched nervously to the folds of my dress.

"'Oh, mother," he whispered, 'I will be good. I won't cry once. Oh, mother, don't throw me into the snow. There was a heavy mist before my eyes, and I hardly recollect what I did. If you had only known what I suffered! My little daughter who nestled closer than ever to my breast; she must be saved, I thought. Must I say what happened? You can guess. My eldest boy died as his brother had died before him.

"Must you hear the rest? I was almost mad now; the roaring of the wolves, the horse, the last cries of my children, the awful thought of seeing my baby torn from my arms, the dread of death— all mingled into a terrible nightmare. I could not move hand nor foot; my eyes were fixed and still I clasped my babe to my chest. I dared not look behind me; but at last, I heard a terrible yell in my ears, and for a second I felt something on my shoulder. Why did I not faint? I turned my head. I saw a wolf with open jaws, clinging by his claws to the back of the sled. He made a half spring at me, missed his hold, and fell back into the snow. Three times he made a fresh spring, three times he missed his hold. The fourth time, he got his claws on the sled again, and there for a few seconds he hung. There was only one chance to dash him back before he could get a firm hold. His claws stuck deep into my fingers, as by force I tried to wrench them from the sled. It was a desperate struggle, and I had almost succeeded, when my baby fell from my arms! From that moment to the time when I first heard the sound of human voices, I can remember nothing. The reins had long since fallen from my hands; I knew the horse was galloping on; but I can recollect no more. I have no conception where we have been or how I got here."

The young woman again covered her face with her hands and burst into a passionate flood of tears. There was an awful silence in the room, broken every now and then by the hysterical sobs of many of the women that stood around. The men trembled, too, and looked steadily on the ground, but did not speak a word. At last, a white-haired woman began to speak some words of consolation in a low, trembling voice.

Immediately the young serf, who had his hatchet still in his hands, strode toward the miserable woman. He was deadly pale and trembled in every limb; the expression in his face had changed suddenly. He glared fiercely at the young woman, and at the old peasant, who was still trying to console her.

"Be still, mother!" he thundered out, "the wretched woman deserves none of your pity."

And then he turned to her.

"Unhappy and most miserable woman! Is it possible that you have done all that you have related? You are a mother, you tell us, and yet you have killed your children one by one. Not one would you spare, not even the boy who prayed to you on his knees, or the baby child who smiled upon your breast. To save your own life you sacrificed theirs, for you had not the courage to die with them. You are unworthy to live!"

There was a shriek in the room and the woman fell at his feet. In an instant the peasants guessed the mad purpose of the young serf. Two of the strongest rushed forward to stop his hand. They were too late. A wild, awful light glittered in the young man's eyes, and with almost supernatural strength he dashed the peasants back. The hatchet whistled through the air and in an instant the unhappy woman was dead at his feet.

Three months after the terrible scene related above, the young serf was brought up before the highest criminal court and charged with willful murder. There was no need to prolong the trial. The young serf was found guilty of murder and condemned to die. But eventually, by the direct command of the emperor, the sentence of the court was reversed, and the young serf was committed to ten years' servitude in Siberia.

12

The Cuckoo's Song

Ten o'clock had just struck in all the clocks in the little town of Heimberg, in the canton of Bern, Switzerland, and a metallic undulation seemed to still vibrate in the air, prolonging itself from house to house, from street to street, to indicate that the morning was advancing. The streets were crowded with passers-by, workmen, peasants, laborers, and idlers, rich and poor. This little town was but a great capital on a small scale. The merchants uncovered their goods and removed the dust of the night. The gossip passed from one door to another in the midst of the universal activity, and each one crying good morning.

"Ten o'clock," cried the big, brawny butcher Herman—whose sponge he vigorously wielded was making the slabs of white marble brilliantly white once more. "Ten o'clock and our neighbor Samuel Stauffer still sleeps! It is astonishing!"

His face, tinged with red hair, with his heavy, square chin and pale blue eyes, expressed, in fact, complete amazement.

"That's so; you are right!" responded Bloch, the grocer, who came out on his doorstep twisting a long piece of paper and leaning forward a little in order to penetrate more materially into the phenomenon which curved and elevated the brows of the butcher like the arches of a bridge. "The broker has not raised one of his shutters and nothing seems to be moving in his house; yet his domestic, Jean Mailer, is habitually an early riser, and this is the first time that I have ever risen before him."

"Bah! What trade could he make this morning? Perhaps the storm of last night hindered his sleeping, and he is making up for it now."

"Oh, what a storm it was," remarked the grocer. "I scarcely closed my eyes; the shutters rattled, and the hinges creaked. All of a sudden: bang! A chimney tumbled into my yard. I have rarely heard such a high wind since I have been in business here."

"Without counting," added the butcher, "the thunder, hail and rain, one could almost say the devil was conducting a dance." And he accentuated his little joke with a loud laugh, which shook his stomach and shoulders so that the fat on his chin and cheeks had terrible convulsions.

"Hush Herman, never say that! It is an evil omen, believe me."

"Oh, what a superstitious fellow you are! One must have a laugh now and then."

"I admit that subject of conversation is repugnant to me, always; for every time that hideous name is mentioned, there is misfortune lurking somewhere." The laugh of the butcher increased at the sight of the pale face of his companion.

"Well, well, you are timid. I wonder what old Samuel is doing."

"Let us knock at his door. What do you say?"

The grocer indicated with his fingers, without budging, the house of Samuel. The butcher, without speaking, directed his steps toward the little shop. It had two floors surmounted by an attic and seemed to bury among the other buildings its pointed roof, covered with tiles. The shop occupied the whole of the ground floor. The wooden shutters solidly fixed by large bars of iron, and the front door with its tight bolts, kept an unaccustomed silence. On the floor above, the blinds stopped up the windows hermetically, and this house with its eyes closed in the midst of the morning bustle assumed an ominous aspect. On the roof the wind vane turned by the wind emitted every now and then a mournful cry, that resembled the moan of a sea gull across the hurricane which agitates the sea.

The butcher struck the bars with his fist and listened to the echo transmitted by the solitary knock through the corridors of the house. He waited a few minutes, then knocked again, and called loudly with his strong voice. No answer. A vague terror stole into his breast and made his heartbeat with quickened motions. He felt under the influence of the silence, broken only by the sad, irritating cry of the weathervanes, and he dared not knock again.

"No answer!" cried Bloch to him from afar.

Then Herman advanced slowly, pushed by curiosity only exceeded by his alarm. "It is extraordinary! I cannot explain it. How is it that neither Samuel nor his servant answer to my call? Could they both be dead? Bloch, I think it is our duty to summon the chief of police. I will send one of my boys. Wait here."

When the police arrived, accompanied by his men, a surgeon, and a locksmith, they were obliged to traverse a dense crowd which increased every minute, surging around like the waters of a river overflowing its banks, and showing an eager desire to find out what was occurring.

The lock was thrown back in a few minutes and the door opened. Everything lent to the mystery. The obscurity gave to the various objects in the shop fantastic shapes. Samuel Stauffer bought and sold everything; furniture collections, novelties, antiques, silver goods and kitchen utensils; each was an article of trade to him. A thick dust was everywhere, blending the colors and softening the angles. The spiders, working without fear, had finished by uniting bronzes, paintings, and crockery with their webs.

The door was guarded by two policemen to prevent the invasion of the curious crowd. The chief, along with the butcher and grocer, both familiar with the household, were followed by the surgeon. They ascended the stairs slowly, one after the other, and arrived in front of the old man's room. They knocked— pure formality. The door, closed only with a latch, offered no resistance. The policeman advanced a few steps and found himself in the most profound obscure darkness. He demanded if someone had brought a light. No one had thought of it.

"Walk straight ahead," said the butcher; "the window is opposite the door. The chief having followed this advice, opened the window, and threw back the blinds, which intercepted the light of day. The light penetrating quickly into the room, lit up a horrible tableau, and a feeling of terror caused those to recoil who stood behind the policeman. The disordered bed was not only messy but trampled. The covers were thrown about and dragged into the center of the room, with two chairs overturned. On the table, soiled by grease which had dripped from the candle, was a carafe half filled with water and a broken glass.

Everything denoted a violent struggle, a terrible resistance, that of a victim against a murderer. In front of the bed— hanging on the wall was one of those clocks called a cuckoo. But what a hideous sight. One of the weighted chains which hung from the cuckoo was wound about the neck of the unfortunate Samuel Stauffer, suspended four inches from the floor. The face already purple, the features inflated and convulsed, showed that all hope was lost. Samuel was dead.

The surgeon hastened to ascertain as soon as the body was stretched on the bed. The iron chain was deeply encrusted in the flesh, making a fearful bloody collar, horrible to see. The hands of the clock, arrested on the face, pointed to three in the morning. There were therefore seven hours that the broker had ceased to live. The motion must have left the clock while the last breath left the lips of the dead man.

Was it murder or suicide? If one judged simply from the inspection of the place, the struggle was startling evidence of murder. The broker had been surprised in his bed, sound asleep; he had resisted as long as his weak body and age would permit. Two chairs overturned, the broken glass, noises which were lost in the storm; the murderer seizing the chain of the cuckoo and strangling the man, leaving him hanging just grazing the floor; this was the theory of the policeman—a theory so plausible that the assistants and even the surgeon listened without dispute.

"If you imagine a suicide," recommenced the policeman, who was warming up to his subject and agitating his arms, "then Samuel Stauffer got upon a chair and, kicking it over with his foot, remained hanging by the neck. It is inadmissible. How can you explain the broken glass? Why two chairs overturned instead of one? Why the disordered state of the bed, the blankets dragged to the foot of the wall, nearly under the clock? Find a connection with the theory of suicide and explain it if you can."

He stopped out of breath. Everyone was silent, regarding the corpse with horror. After a minute the surgeon said: "Pardon me, sir. But from where came the assassin, and how could he have opened the door?"

"You think it was suicide," said the policeman, tartly.

"But," said the big butcher, coming forward, "Samuel Stauffer had a servant."

"The servant, ah! I had forgotten him," said the policeman, with a triumphal regard towards the surgeon. "Quick, go and find him!"

Herman and the chief precipitated themselves into the room which was occupied by Jean Muller. In one corner the domestic of the young man of twenty-five, half-dressed, was crouched on the floor like some wild animal, holding his head in his hands, without voice, without life, haggard and appearing to be under a terrible impression.

"What are you doing?" asked the policeman, who dared not approach.

No reply. Muller did not budge. They assisted him to rise and supported him under the arms. He let them do it with complete indifference. Herman handed him his jacket and supported on each side the young man was conducted into the presence of his murdered master. When he recognized the room of Samuel Stauffer, a trembling seized his limbs and by a quick motion he attempted to escape, but the iron hand of the butcher stopped the despairing effort. The chief of police turned his head; his suspicions were beginning to be confirmed more and more. Brought before the bed opposite the corpse, he regarded it stupidly, but without fear. It was not until he turned and saw the fatal chain that any terror seemed to possess him. He trembled violently, his teeth shattered and falling on his knees, he appeared to ask for mercy. But not a sound issued from his lips; he made only the most incomprehensible gesture.

"The boy was not dumb before?" asked the chief. "He spoke without doubt?"

"Perfectly," replied Bloch. "Go ahead, Jean, answer! Tell us who killed your master?"

The servant did not reply.

"This man appears to be unable to speak," said the surgeon, who examined Muller attentively, "it may be that this murder has struck him in a terrible and unexpected manner. We have examples of such cases among the witnesses of harrowing scenes."

"That is well enough for witnesses, but do you think the

same effect can be produced on an assassin once his crime is accomplished?" asked the policeman.

"That, I do not know."

"But will the law admit this weak circumstance? We can judge of it very soon. You must know that mental derangement and dumbness are two great ways of vindicating culprits. I have seen criminals pretend insanity for entire months, in such a manner as to defeat science and physicians and avoid the capital punishment that they merited."

"I cannot, however, believe it a crime," responded the surgeon.

"In waiting for the trial, the law which I represent, and which ought to protect society, arrests and imprisons Jean Muller, accused until further proof of the crime of homicide, intentional and perhaps premeditated, on the person of his master, Samuel Stauffer, merchant and broker is obtained."

The servant, Jean, let himself be led by the policeman without manifesting any emotion. The police surrounded him to protect him from the insults of the mob. The cuckoo clock to which the unfortunate man was hung was carried to the prison and disappeared behind the heavy door and massive bolts of the jail. On the day after they buried Samuel Stauffer, his goods were sold at auction, for he left no will or heirs. But they could not find a purchaser for the house, which was closed and passed immediately as a sinister and dangerous dwelling. It was strictly avoided when night fell and often the grocer Bloch, who dwelt opposite, would shiver with agony between his sheets, believing he heard sounds coming from behind the blinds of the late Samuel Stauffer.

Two months sped by— two long months— during which

life had retaken its habitual course— two months in which a thousand incidents of the act had accumulated slowly on the terrible event which took place the night of the storm. The little house at last found a purchaser when they had almost despaired of ever finding one. It was a mysterious old peddler, by the name of Elias Wolfmann, who announced his intention to take the business of Samuel Stauffer. But he had not opened shop yet.

The little town of Heimberg was in a perfect flutter of excitement. The people crowded and pressed around the courthouse. Jean Muller was about to be tried and the curiosity which had been increasing day by day had now reached its culminating point.

Jean had not yet spoken. His lawyer himself had not been able to draw him from his obstinate silence which seemed almost supernatural. What could he hope for? The law face to face with the horror of the crime would be pitiless toward such stubbornness unless the insanity of the unfortunate man could be proven, and it was this course, which had been adopted by his lawyer who not only saw no other way to save him, but he had come to believe it himself.

The trial began: the judge and jurymen took their places. Hanging on the wall was the fatal cuckoo. It had become an instrument of death— a certain proof of the crime. There it was: a silent, sinister witness marking the hour of three. This clock was a little larger than those that are usually made, which explains how it could support the weight of a man. A sort of niche in the woodwork hid the bird from sight, who sung the hour. The public could not look at it without fear. Everyone felt the influence of the mystery, and all thought that the trial would not throw much light on it, unless the accused could be made to speak. The prisoner was ordered to appear. The crowd swayed like a field of wheat in the wind. All heads were turned toward the same place the little door by which Jean Muller entered.

Every sound ceased and a silence like death weighed on this multitude so restless, so tumultuous an instant before. Muller advanced between two guards, tall, thin and fair, with a gentle look; his eyes troubled and his head lowered. He walked without knowing what he did. Not a sound escaped his lips; his glance was fixed on the ground. The witnesses gave their testimony— it all tended towards a crime. He was alone in the house with his master; he was hidden when they made the discovery; he had neither confessed nor denied the murder. One question alone remained to decide his fate. Had he committed the murder in cold blood or in a fit of insanity?

Jean Muller had not raised his eyes. He seemed neither to hear nor understand. It was like a torch extinguished. Suddenly in one corner of the hall there arose a murmur, which increased little by little till it reached the front ranks. A man traversed the crowd, using his fists and elbows to make himself a free passage, and arriving near the prisoner he looked at him with a strange sneer, then leaping lightly over the railing which separated the tribunal and the public he addressed himself to the judges.

"Gentlemen, will you permit me to make a test to recall this unfortunate man to reason? I am called Elias Wolfmann, Your Honor. I sold this clock to the late Samuel Stauffer and just recently purchased his residence."

A shiver ran through his hearers at this declaration; the curiosity was redoubled; every ear was wide open. Wolfmann was a tall, angular person with a yellow beard floating in two points from his chin; his nose was sharp, and his small gray eyes were hidden beneath the bushy eyebrows; a continual sneer hovered around the corners of his month. He wore a long coat reaching to his ankles gathered at the waist with a wide belt and immense brass buckle. His costume was not flattering and the resident of Heimberg did not associate with him willingly. It was with great interest that they looked at him, detailing his dress and scrutinizing his features. He appeared false and perfidious.

"I ask but one thing," he said, "the permission to put in motion this clock."

It was granted. Then mounting a chair, he put in motion the pendulum. At the fourth stroke the niche opened, and the cuckoo appeared on the threshold, and singing three times announced the hour. It had hardly finished when music hidden in the body of the clock played the *"Rauz des Voches"* but in a manner so piercing and weird that it awed everyone. At the moment when the cuckoo rang, Jean raised himself like one awakened from a dream; he gazed at the clock with arms outstretched, and his mouth open, expressing an awful fear and trying to cover his face with his hands. The clock had resumed its monotonous tick-tock and the hands moved mechanically around its face.

When the music ceased, Jean stood up and said with a steady voice, looking at the judges, "What do you want? Why have you arrested me? I am innocent. I will swear it. My master killed himself. I am saying nothing but the truth. The night of the murder was a fearful one, as you all know," said the young man, "a storm mixed with rain, hail, and thunder, so that nothing which transpired at my masters could be heard in the neighborhood. Samuel Stauffer entered the house at nine o'clock in the evening carrying this clock under his arm, and it was I who hung it solidly to the wall of his own room, opposite his bed. He seemed enchanted, with his bargain, and talked of it incessantly. At ten o'clock I assisted him to regulate the cuckoo and to put it in motion. At half past ten it struck for the first time and played the air which you have just heard. I was helping Samuel Stauffer to disrobe. He turned to me abruptly as if something had struck him.

"'Do you not think that music strange?' said he.

"I told him effectually that it had shaken my nerves a little at which he laughed heartily. 'Well,' he explained, 'go to bed; that will calm you.'

"I left him alone and ascended into my room just above his, where, owing to the age of the house, a piece of displaced plastering enabled me to see all that passed in my master's room. I was preparing for bed when 11 o'clock struck and the music began again. I heard my master turn in his bed, and it disturbed me so that I cast a glance into his room. He was standing in front of the clock, a candle in his hand, gazing at it with an anxious air as if the sound irritated him.

"I went to bed and in ten minutes I slept profoundly. The time flew by and 3 o'clock had just struck when I heard an explosion of furious cries beneath me. It was then that I witnessed a horrible spectacle. Samuel Stauffer, foaming at the mouth, his eyes bulging from their sockets, shook his fist at the clock, crying, 'you will cause my death, but you will not ring anymore!' In an instant he leaped upon a chair and passed one of the chains around his neck, pushed the seat from under him and remained hanging. The clock stopped instantly at 3 o'clock. I looked at him, unable to help him. I had a frightful desire to imitate his example. Had I gone below, it would have been certain death. I do not remember anything more until today.

"That is the whole truth gentlemen, and you must have felt the strange impression produced by the song of this cuckoo."

As he finished, the half hour struck and held anew everyone with its inexplicable power. The members of the jury could thus judge by their own sensations the truth of its recital made by the accused. The jury retired to deliberate. When they entered, the verdict was simply the acquittal of Jean Muller. The verdict was received with applause.

Wolfmann was brought before the bar. "You will be conducted to the gates of the city and forbidden to ever step foot inside again. The price of the house bought by you will be refunded, and this infernal clock shall be publicly burned."

The hour was about to strike but the movement was immediately stopped by a nearby guard. Conducted outside the walls, Wolfmann never reappeared, and the cuckoo was burned on the spot. The grocer Bloch was certain that the devil constructed the clock, and his neighbor Herman, more credulous now, dared not contradict him.

The little house of Samuel Stauffer was given to Jean Muller, who let it fall into ruins. He replaced it with a new building, with everybody in town assisting him. The people of Heimberg would go to his shop to listen to the history of the death of the old peddler and the terrible song of the cuckoo.

* 9 7 9 8 2 1 8 0 9 5 7 8 9 *